Minor Larceny

John Lloyd

Contents

Disclaimer

This is a work of fiction. Names, characters, places and incidents either are products of the author's imagination or are used fictitiously. Any resemblance to actual events or locales or persons, living or dead, is entirely coincidental.

Dedication

For my father-in-law and good friend Mike Upham. I'm sure he would have enjoyed this story.

Acknowledgments

Florence Lloyd for capturing the innocence of Truffle on the cover drawing, Flo you're a sweetheart.

Oliver Lloyd and Phil Taylor for your guidance on various aspects of the Law, thanks to you both.

Those kind neighbours who acted for me as Beta Readers.

About the Author

John has a lot in common with the principal character in this story. Born shortly following the Second World War, he grew up in middle England, and apart from a few years spent living and working in South Africa on a work assignment, the Midlands is where he currently lives. With four sons, a daughter, a wife, and a dog called Truffle, time flies by.

Chapter 1: A Beer at The Bar

It was a Wednesday evening in the middle of November, a chilly, drizzly, miserable night outside, but who cares? I was in the comfortable warmth of the room, settled back into my seat next to an old cast iron radiator located just spitting distance away from the bar. It was my chosen corner spot, furthest away from the entrance doorway so as not to suffer any wintery drafts from people entering or leaving the pub and set back into a small alcove away from the slightly larger main seating area of the 'Snug.'

The story does and doesn't really start here, I'm not trying to over complicate the tale, just attempting to help you, the reader, understand the interplay of relationships and the unforeseen circumstances leading up to the critical situation that I, and others, found ourselves in as the real story plays out. One more thing, Minor Larceny is a strange title for a story that unfolds into a truly horrible crime, but it relates to the days of innocence which played their part in leading to the final outcome. So, I ask that you bear with me and let me unfold the tale of how things happened, in my own way.

Going for a beer at my local pub on a Wednesday evening had only recently become a part of my weekly routine, and tonight, as chance would have it, the place where I preferred to sit had been unoccupied on my arrival. I shouldn't really claim it as 'my spot.' I had only recently deigned to visit the pub once a week, and even then, I never stayed longer than an hour or so. Just long enough for one, or occasionally two, pints of my preferred drink, Guinness.

Recovering from my second bout of Coronavirus, this latest episode hitting me towards the end of October, had effectively curtailed my newly acquired pub routine by a couple of weeks. Tonight was the inaugural return to my 'bad ways.' Well not strictly true, I'm sure that one pint of Guinness a week could not be considered a truly bad habit.

Initially and hopefully I thought my latest bout of COVID might have only been a spell of 'man-flu.' It didn't seem to have been as bad as the first time I had gone down with it. Not such a sore throat compared with my first encounter, just a cough this time and generally feeling rough. But the test kit swab, rotated uncomfortably at the back of my throat until I gagged, before it then being twizzled around up my right nostril, had successfully destroyed that misconception and once again sentenced me to a week or so spent in isolation. The dreaded lurgy had struck again.

This, the second encounter I had experienced with the virus, could, I was pretty certain, be attributed to my wife, Sally. She had begun to exhibit similar symptoms, sore throat, and dry cough, a few days earlier than me and had also tested positive, so - 'ipso facto' - the finger of blame pointed fairly and squarely at her.

Still, so many people had suffered or were still suffering, far greater and sadder experiences than my mean encounter with the virus, and once again, I was over it, at least for now. Feeling I fully deserved a pint of the black stuff as a welcome way to line the back of my throat and celebrate my release from self-isolation. So here I sat, back in the pub that I had only recently determined to be 'my local.'

I did have a choice, there being two pubs in the village where I lived, but one, The White Hart, an old, thatched building dating back to the 1640's, had suffered extensive fire damage about a year or so back and had, until very recently, been out of commission. Thatched roofs and fire do not 'go down' well together, they had more factually 'gone up' in flames, and the building itself had been more or less reduced to a shell.

Being a listed building, The White Hart had been required to be brought back to its former glory and, after what seemed to be quite an extended period, while it was undergoing repair and rethatching, had only recently returned back into service, following an extensive renovation.

Of the two pubs, The White Hart was, when running normally, what I would term a 'real village pub,' with a dart board and a regular crowd of drinkers, all of whom seemed to know one another, laugh loudly, and had the tendency to shout rather than talk. The shouting could readily be explained as being something of a necessity because when everyone else in the pub is talking loudly, shouting becomes the only way of getting heard.

The Queens Crown, the other pub in the village and the one I was currently favouring, was also a building with heritage. It, too, dates back to the 17th century but was more of a combination of pub, restaurant, and hotel.

In terms of proximity to where I lived, both pubs were, though in slightly different directions, about five to ten minutes' walking distance. So there is not much to choose from in travel time to journey to either. Both allowed dogs into their bar areas, another factor of importance to be taken into consideration for me, and both had Guinness on tap. So I guess I was spoilt for choice.

I found that I enjoyed a pint of Guinness - more so than traditional beers of late - I hadn't been too keen on the taste in my younger years, but I guess tastes change as you get older. Sally had told me that it was probably a result of having too many hot curries over the years, searing my tastebuds. I think she was joking.

Of the two pubs, I had settled for my now regular Wednesday night drink, on The Queens Crown. The decision had not being too great a challenge really, seeing as how The White Hart had taken itself out of the running, since it had been closed until recently with the fire damage.

So there I sat, a pint of Guinness in one hand, mobile phone in the other, staring intently at my small screen, ignoring everyone else, and relaxing in my self-imposed exile while enjoying a quiet drink. It was an activity, or more correctly, a lack of activity, that I was currently sharing with only two other drinkers presently occupying the Snug area of the pub with me. We were all men in our later years, all quietly ignoring one another, each totally immersed in and mesmerised by the small phone screens that demanded our attention.

Occasionally one of us would put our drink down to momentarily tap into the keyboard on our phone, but that just about amounted to the full extent of the Snug room activity.

There was no excuse for my lack of participative activity. My attention was focused on solving today's Wordle challenge. It was something that had recently become a nightly habit, whether at home or in the pub, as was the case at present, and constituted a viable excuse for me not having to interact, in all but the narrowest of terms, with either of the two other old fogies I shared the room with. Oh, don't get me wrong, we smiled and nodded to one another from time to time, usually when one of us got up to go to the bar or visit the 'Gents,' but that was about the full extent of our socialising.

I had already placed my new fleece-lined thermal gloves and old woolly beanie hat on the radiator to absorb some of the warmth, all ready for my journey home.

This had now become my preferred place to sit when visiting the pub, a habit I had started enjoying now most Wednesday evenings between nine and ten. I had claimed my spot in the Snug about eight or nine weeks ago, and, apart from my recent spell out with the illness, it had once again become the centre point of my Wednesday evening routine. I was as snug as a bug in a rug, so to say, sinking down into my seat - welcoming the warmth and enjoying the relaxed solitude.

I wasn't even too bothered about the risk of anyone pinching my spot near the bar. I'm not that paranoid about where I sit, anywhere will do, and this side of the pub was never too busy.

The beer was fine, Jason, the barman, and the other bar staff all seemed a friendly lot, and over the years, on the few odd occasions that I had found myself having a beer there, I felt that, of the two, this pub better suited my temperament and preference for enjoying my own company.

Truth be told, I am quite happy to join in and enjoy the company of others, but I also prefer that to be on my terms and at my timing. I'm also quite happy spending periods of time on my own, nothing too prolonged, just the occasional relaxed, comfortable hour in my own enjoyable solitude. Sally had once, jokingly I believe, said I would have coped well with prison life.

The Queens Crown, with its mixed role as a restaurant and bar, seemed to have determined the character and atmosphere of the place. For someone just going out for a drink in the evening, I never felt it had a 'bar feel.' It was more the sort of place where people tended to talk quietly, keeping their conversations within their group and generally keeping to themselves. Difficult to put my finger on it, but I guess the pub just lacked that loud and lively atmosphere necessary to generate or attract a regular beer-drinking crowd.

Funnily enough, seeing the purpose for which Sally had set me off with the task of making new friends in the village was probably the principal reason I had chosen to use this pub as my preferred 'local.' That and, of course, the fact that The White Hart had been closed for the past nine months or so while its fire damage was being sorted out.

I should add here that, if it wasn't already apparent, I had not fully 'bought into' Sally's insistence that I needed to go out to a pub to find new friends locally. I was more than happy to keep my own company and just meet up with a few old friends on more of a monthly, or two monthly basis, like I did when a group of the guys from my old rugby club met up for a curry.

As for making new friends, I told myself that I was happy for that to come about in its own time and occur naturally, if it ever did, by taking a more relaxed approach to that sort of advice. However, in truth, I recognised that I was just being lazy when it came to having to make an effort to socialise with strangers.

Certainly, in the Snug tonight, I felt no compulsion, or even the slightest inclination, towards starting up a friendship with either of these two other old fogies, each sitting there staring at their phones. A feeling I am sure they would have shared. Sometimes it is good to just enjoy doing sod all.

I wasn't really what you would call a 'drinking man,' at least not since my days of club rugger forty years or so ago. Don't get me wrong, I like the odd beer now and again, and am partial to a brandy when I settle down in the evening to watch the television. The only problem there is that alcohol before bed, Sally tells me, makes me snore, and although that was not something I found particularly annoying, she apparently does.

Sally works late at the college in Leamington on Wednesdays. She teaches students Business Studies and doesn't normally get home until around 9pm. So going out for a drink at the local pub on those Wednesday evenings where she works late seemed like a convenient habit to adopt, and, as it was at her insistence, I had no problems from that point of view.

'For God's sake, go out and make some friends in the village, you miserable sod. You're stuck in here on your own most of the day, either watching the bloody television or listening to Audible stories on your phone! Get out more, get a life, you're turning into an old man!'

'You may not have noticed,' I had pointed out, 'I am now in my mid-seventies, which I believe actually qualifies me as officially being an 'old man,' and I regularly take Truffle out for her walkies.' It was a feeble defence, and deep down, I had to accept there was a modicum of truth in what she was saying, I was letting the remainder of my life slowly slip by me. But I still felt the need to put up some token of defence.

'And I do the Food Bank Collection.' A weak retort I have to admit, that sounded pitiful even to me.

The Food Bank Collection meant driving around the village shops, Sainsbury's, the Co-op, the Post Office, and a One Stop shop and collecting food donations, then delivering them to a nearby village church where they were sorted by a team of volunteers - all charming and caring middle-aged ladies I noticed, doing their bit for the community – preparing the food orders ready to be sent out to the allotted distribution centres.

Collection of the food donations from the contributing shops was again undertaken by volunteers, all retired old timers like me willing to 'do their bit' by sacrificing a couple of hours of retirement boredom a month to a worthy cause, and because there are, thankfully, a fair few of us doing the collection, it meant I was only called on to play my part as a delivery driver, for an hour or two, no more than once a month.

But I wasn't going to win this argument, not that we were arguing, just failing to agree. Or more on my part, just failing to admit Sally was right.

So meekly following Sal's insistence, like the good obedient husband I am, I journeyed out to the pub for an hour or so early on a Wednesday evening, finding it to be not to be too much of an imposition at all.

The short walk from our house to the pub, and the journey back, also ticked a couple of 'to-do' boxes for me. It contributed to my 'Ten thousand steps a day goal,' something I religiously measured on my Fitbit watch, whilst also satisfying Sally's requirement, at least on the face of it, that I mingle more with the locals.

For a short time, the trip to the pub also addressed the evening walk with my dog Truffle need, but not for long. I'll come to that shortly.

So with two months of pubbing under my belt and fulfilling my Wednesday night pub visit duty, I was beginning to feel like a 'regular' and even the barman, with a name badge telling me he was Jason, now greeted me by name and remembered my preference for a pint of Guinness even before I asked.

As I mentioned, at first, I began my trips to the pub taking my dog Truffle, a Dorkie - a cross between a miniature Dachshund and a Yorkshire Terrier - with me, initially this ticked another box 'to-do' box by making sure she got her evening 'walkies.'

I will properly introduce Truffle at this point, she is a friendly little dog, about the size of a cat, but with shorter legs, who loves being the centre of attention and expects everyone who passes by to want to stroke her - which, because she is such a friendly little dog and as cute-as-cute-can-be, they usually do.

Unfortunately though, like many little dogs, especially those of the terrier classification, she has a bad case of 'small dog syndrome.' If she happens to find herself in an enclosed space, or any seated area where there is another dog present, whether in the pub, a cafe, or anywhere else where people go to settle down and relax with their dogs, she yaps continuously and loudly at what she considers to be her rivals for attention. It is not a friendly bark, either. Her behaviour would best be described as being 'extremely aggressive,' in a yapping sort of way, towards whatever innocent pooch had dared to enter 'her space.'

Over the years, in such situations, Sal and I have tried all manner of means to divert her attention from those other innocent hounds, which generally sit quietly staring back, as if bewildered by my annoyingly embarrassing little dog, but nothing seems to work. It has been suggested, by well-meaning people, that we try turning her head away from the other dog, or 'try picking her up,' but to no avail. She just barks, snarls, and barks and barks. You get the picture.

For some reason, for which again I can offer no explanation, Truffle has a particular aversion to huskies and poodles and, as chance would have it, when we first began our visits to The Queens Crown, a gentleman, of around my age, always seemed to be sitting there, in the 'Snug,' with his beautiful and rather large husky.

It was again one of those situations where the husky's owner and I would exchange tight smiles anticipating what we both knew was shortly to happen, the resulting dog confrontation being the predictable outcome. It would start with Truffle giving a low-pitched growling grumble from the back of her throat, leading on to a full-out snarling and barking fit. If dogs could be said to smirk, that would best describe the look on the husky's face as she sat quietly staring silently back at my little companion.

None of my attempts to calm Truffle ever worked, and eventually, I would be embarrassed to the point of having to down whatever I had left of my pint of Guinness and end my evening out at the pub so peace and tranquillity could return.

'Aggressive little bugger, isn't she?' following one such occurrence, Jason, the barman, had said to me.

'You should have called her Wolf.' I failed to see the humour in that, but he seemed to think it was hilarious. I just smiled, but it had set the barmaid off giggling, so I guess she at least must have thought his remark bordered on the edge of being mildly amusing.

From then on, following two or three similarly embarrassing barking encounters with the husky, I stopped taking Truffle (aka Wolf) with me on my pub outings.

Whenever I went into the pub, from then on, either one of the bar staff, usually but not exclusively Jason - would think it amusing to ask. 'Not got Wolf with you tonight, then?'

It was easiest on such occasions just to use a false smile as a response. That's what sometimes passes for village humour around our way, and I have to accept it. I just had to roll with it, after all it wasn't malicious or meant to cause any upset.

So, there I sat on this, a particularly chilly night, all alone with my Guinness, phone out and Wordle ready, but with no dog to keep me company. Again, supposedly making new friends, but not really making much progress or in truth expending any effort in that direction.

The lighting in my corner of the bar wasn't too good. Just bright enough to see what I was drinking but useless for reading anything without holding it up to the dusty wall-mounted lights.

That suited me, I was happy in my own company, there wasn't anything in particular that I wanted to read anyway, and my mobile had its own backlight if I did.

It being the middle of the week, as usual, there were only a couple of other solo drinkers in the Snug, and of course, that beautiful grey and white husky with its ice blue eyes, all quietly enjoying our own company. From where I sat I could see through into the main bar and restaurant area, where the lighting was much brighter. It was a little noisier than usual through there tonight, it looked like there might be the beginnings of a 'hen party' enjoying a meal together before they took off for one of the nightclubs in Leamington or Coventry. Unusual for a Wednesday night, I thought, still probably better to have purged all the alcohol out of your system a few days before the wedding, I guess, rather than turning up on 'the big day' with a hangover.

The likelihood was I thought that there would be snow overnight. I gave a little shiver, burrowing further down into my fleece-padded jacket. Nursing my Guinness, I reached over to rest my free arm on the radiator that was valiantly trying to throw out some heat into the surrounding area.

I guess it would be nice if we had a little bit of snow over Christmas, I can't remember when we had last had a 'White Christmas', but the festivities were still five weeks away, and I wasn't holding out too much hope for snow, not here in the Midlands anyway.

'Snuggled up' in the Snug. Happy in my self-imposed solitude, I let my mind wander back through time. Smiling to myself, I brought back foggy memories of people and places only half-remembered. On balance, my journey through life so far had been relatively untroubled. A few ups and downs, like most people. Two marriages, over a span of fifty years or so, had given me a raft of experiences and a handful of children, all of whom were now grown out of childhood and busy creating their own life stories.

This was where my thoughts rambled, wandering through half-recalled glimpses, snapshots of earlier times, people I had met along my own life journey, some I had called friends. Years and distance had diluted most, if not all, of those friendships to the point where they had dwindled into insignificance, just foggy ghosts from the past.

Memory is such a fickle friend, some things - minor things of little importance from years back I can remember in detail, others - more relevant and useful for my life today - are a different story. I can recall the licence plate on the car, a black Triumph Mayflower, my father drove back in the early 1950's - KWK995. However, when it comes to parking my current car in a metered car park and needing to register it into RingGo, I invariably end up either getting out of the car to look and remind myself of the licence plate number or, most frequently searching through the 'Contacts App' on my iPhone, where I keep the registration number stored, surprise-surprise, filed away under an app headed 'Car'.

I gave some thought to the guys I had played rugby with over the years. An important part of my younger days. You could put together a full team from the ghosts of those I had known and who had passed away since then.

After another swallow of Guinness, I definitely was beginning to sink from contented apathy into a more morbid 'down mood'. I don't know where this self-pitying was coming from. I tried to recapture back my earlier mood, but that wasn't working, so I decided to just ride with it. It would pass, sometime - I told myself - it was alright to think back to past times, remembering the mistakes, missed opportunities and lost friendships as well as the good times.

Awareness hit me of the reduced role I now, since retirement, played in other people's lives. Gradually allowing my morbid mood to take a firmer hold of my contentment and shift it along the satisfaction scale into the realms of doldrums.

Wasn't retirement supposed to be the reward and happy conclusion to all those years of work?

Not working quite so well for me, three years after fully retiring from my office-based job, with a 'shed full' of good ideas for retirement that I had determined would keep me active and motivated, and I was bored to death and feeling like a 'spare part' just waiting for life to have done with me.

I was beginning to accept that Sally might be right. I do need an interest, a distraction, a project, a reason for re-engaging my brain. Nothing quite so menial as finding new friends in the neighbourhood by going down to the local pub, but something more substantial. And not just another 'great idea for another day,' I needed something now. Something I could actively engage with. A challenge to take on and master. I had to get the blood flowing again. I wasn't ready to hang up my boots yet. Too many of those old rugby teammates had died of age-related illnesses in recent years, and I wasn't ready to join that ghost team in the sky quite yet.

One more sip of beer and a new determination set in - I would take hold of the reins and bloody well do something to 'get the train back on the rails.'

The influence of alcohol - beer talking? Certainly easier said than done, 'make something happen' - But what?

'Who cares what? Just bloody well, do something.'

Someone in the main bar had put some money in the jukebox, and in the background, I could just make out the mellow tones of Bill Withers singing an old favourite of mine, 'Lean on Me.'

'...you've got a friend, someone, to lean on', the words of the song nudging my thoughts along a different track.

An idea began taking shape, pointing towards one possible approach I maybe could explore. Not finding new friends - turn that thought around - why not finding some old friends?

Why not see if I could locate and possibly meet up with again, or at least make contact with, an old friend? I would grab one of my past memories and see if I could create some fun, challenge, and purpose by following it through to create a 'now-time' experience. Why not? What harm could it do? Just give it a go. Where to start?

'Well, why not,' I reasoned with myself, 'take it right back to the beginning, literally? Take one of my earliest memories and see if I could make a connection with someone who had once been important to me but with whom I had since lost contact. Keep it simple, just find them, get in touch, hear how their 'life's journey' so far had been, and, if appropriate and circumstances were right, see if we could meet up and maybe reignite our friendship.

I was beginning to warm to the idea. It could be fun - like playing detective. A search journey at my own pace, in whatever direction my investigation took me. If it led nowhere, then there was nothing to lose, and no one other than me would be any the wiser.

I closed my eyes, took a long pull on my pint, and began to search back through time, revisiting half-forgotten memories, shadows of the past, replaying my early life stories, trying to reconjure past experiences and people I had known long ago.

Chapter 2 - Julie Bishop

February 1954 to August 1954

My earliest memory stretches back to the early 1950's, not so much a memory, more incomplete snapshots of one or two isolated happenings back then. I would have been four years old and in my last Spring and Summer before I started school, in September of that year.

Primary School, where all the big kids went, and one day not too far off, when just that little bit older, I thought I would also be going to do whatever it was they did inside those grey single-story corrugated panel Nissen huts.

Not that I gave it much thought at the time; back then, today was today, and there were plenty of exciting adventures to live, waste dumps and bomb craters to explore, and dens to make in the gardens and fields close by.

I remember my father wasn't around too much in those days. He had, during the war, been a Chief Petty Officer in the Royal Navy and, since then, I assume, had held a similar rank in the Royal Naval Reserves.

I didn't really understand what a Chief Petty Officer was or what his role would be, but he had a flat peaked officer's hat, and I thought that must have made him something like a Sergeant in the army. I might be wrong, but anyway, whatever his role, it seemed as if he was forever being required, even now five years after the war had ended, to disappear for the odd weekend or so on some sort of training programme routine.

I still remember how proud I felt seeing him as he strode off down the street with his duffle bag slung over his shoulder. It felt great that all our neighbours could see him in his navy uniform, on his way to catch a bus or a train, off to some secret place, who knows where.

My dad had gifted me the nickname 'Chilli,' which makes perfect sense now for someone like me with the surname of Pepper, but back then - when chilli peppers were a rarity in the UK - very few people in the Midlands, where we lived, would have understood the association. I guess it must have been his service time in the navy that gave my dad a wider knowledge of spicy foods than was then the norm in post-war Coventry.

In the early 1950's most people in our neighbourhood would have assumed it was 'Chilly,' not Chilli, and somehow falsely associated it with the weather or temperature - that is, of course, if they ever bothered to think about it. Anyway, the nickname stuck Chilli, not John - my real name, the one on my passport - has been what friends, relatives, and even my teachers at school, have always known me as.

Thinking back to those old school days, the only time I ever had to answer the name John Pepper was at the morning class register call. If someone had called out 'John' to me in the street, I would have assumed they were calling someone else.

Anyway - our house was to the west side of Coventry, on the outskirts of the city, a city that had undergone quite heavy war-time damage from Luftwaffe bombings. The city centre was still being cleared of rubble from the bombing raids and was busy rebuilding housing and shops.

Over 4,000 homes, as well as the factories the Luftwaffe were targeting, had been destroyed in Coventry on that fateful evening in November 1940, and over 500 people had died in a raid lasting over ten hours. But our house in Rothesay Avenue was far enough away from those areas that suffered the worst of the bomb damage. Those few bomb craters here and there that were close enough for my pals and me to happily journey to, were definitely places for exploration and excitement.

I first met Julie Bishop late one morning when I think - another memory snapshot - I was standing on an upturned bucket in my back garden. The fences separating adjacent house gardens were generally a mishmash of different constructions, some wire and some unpainted wood, smelling strongly of creosote. It's interesting how the memory of a smell like creosote can linger with you years - no decades - after the time of the memory.

The height of the fences was also a mix, some five or six feet high, others just waist high, allowing people to see over and gossip with the neighbours when hanging out the family's washing on their weathered grey cotton string washing lines.

The wooden fence to the back garden of our house, as I recall, was of this smaller waist high type, not high at all really, but even so for a four - 'but nearly five-year-old' - I still needed an upturned bucket to stand on so as to see into the next yard, or over the gate leading onto the 'back entry.'

The 'back entry' to our house was shared with those houses on Elm Tree Avenue whose rear gardens backed onto ours. This meant we got the sun in our backyard in the morning, and they got the sun in theirs in the afternoon. Most of the houses had their own wooden garage, tool, or coal shed, at the bottom of their gardens - no two garages or sheds looked the same - and all had garden gates leading onto the narrow tarmac private access drive - colloquially known to all living there as the 'back entry.'

One Saturday or Sunday - it must have been one weekend day because my Mum wasn't at work - I was standing on an upturned bucket at my back gate, defending my garden from a marauding tribe of attacking Apache

Indians. Shooting at the attackers over my gate, then ducking down to avoid their pretend arrows. It was when I looked up from one of these attacks that I spotted a small girl standing in the 'back entry,' stroking and cuddling a small furry bundle with a long stringy tail. I say small girl, but I suppose, thinking back on it, she must have been about my height. However, to be fair, I guess I wasn't very tall back then, so I'm right to say she was small.

Picturing her now, in my mind's eye, she had long mousy brown hair tied back in a single plaited ponytail and was wearing a grubby grey and white gingham cotton dress, I suppose, short greyish white ankle socks and, like me, scuffed black leather sandals. I think, and again it's how I now remember it; most of the kids in the street all seemed to wear either black pumps or leather T-bar sandals in those days.

After more or less seventy years, I think it is quite understandable that l can't recall the exact conversation we had back then, but it is reasonable to assume it must have gone somewhat along the lines of what follows.

'What you got there?' I would have shouted over the gate, pointing at whatever it was she was holding.

'It's my new pet rat.' She would have snapped back.

'It's dead,' I said, 'It's not moving.'

'No,' she held it by its neck and pushed it towards me, 'look, it's smiling, it must be alive.'

She was right, I could see its front teeth, it was smiling.

'What are you going to do with it?'

'I am going to feed it, so it will get well again, and I can play with it.' she said.

'Let's show it to my Mum, she will know what to feed it.'

And so we did.

I opened the back gate to my garden, and the girl, me, and the furry bundle went into the kitchen to show the pet rat to my Mum.

My mother's reaction wasn't quite what either the girl or I were expecting!

'Jesus Christ,' Mum screamed. 'It's a dead rat.'

When she was angry, my mother's Welsh accent noticeably became quite pronounced, and back then, as I recall it through the fog of time, it was 'High Cardiff'.

We tried explaining about the rat's smile, but it 'cut no water.'

'It's a dead rat, and it's full of bloody germs; you've got to get rid of it and bloody quick,' my Mum shrieked 'put it in the outside dustbin now Chilli, and then you and your pal get back in here and wash your hands, straight away!'

There was no point in arguing with my Mum when she was in that sort of mood. We did as we were told, and that was pretty much the end of that little story, other than for the fact that for the next week or so, until the dustbin men came to collect the rubbish, the little girl - who I now knew to be called Julie - and I revisited the bin on more than a few occasions to check if the rat had moved at all since we put it there. I think we even brought one or two of the other kids, from the neighbourhood, into my back garden to see our dead rat.

The single, most positive result of this shared encounter was that Julie and I were to become best friends, and for the next six months or so, we always set out to play with one another. She wasn't my only friend, nor I hers. I vaguely remember two or three other children who we would occasionally play with, but I can't recall their names, so I guess they ranked lower in my memory than my friendship with Julie. With plenty of boys to play with, it seemed strange, looking back, that my best friend was a girl. However, a girl she definitely was, but Julie was something special. She was more than just a girl, she was my pal, and maybe it was her, not me, that chose the 'priority of friendship' ranking.

A definite factor, looking back on our games, escapades, and adventures back then, was that Julie was quite a tearaway with a clear mind of her own, even if sometimes I felt she was a bit too bossy. I can look back on it now, seventy years or so, and see that she certainly met all the requirements needed to tick the boxes, in anyone's mind, as being a 'tomboy.'

Together we were Tonto and the Lone Ranger. Me being the Lone Ranger, of course, because she had long hair like a 'Red Injun'... In my mind's eye, I can still visualise Julie with her elasticated snake buckle belt fastened around her head and a pigeon feather, or if there was no feather to be found, a plume of pampas grass from her front garden tucked into the belt around her head.

I would wear a black cardboard cut-out mask, the type that just covers your eyes, and a cowboy belt with a cap gun in my holster - so we were both dressed for the part.

I remember I also used to like to play Zorro with a garden cane as a sword, as it gave me the chance to wear my mask again. But I'm not too sure Julie was so keen on playing 'second fiddle' as Bernardo, the hero's mute 'sidekick,' all the time.

When not cowboys and Indians, we were British soldiers fighting the Germans and the Japs. We were police bobbies catching robbers and 'knights in armour.' My front garden gate became a castle wall; the water ditch in the wasteland near the primary school at the end of 'our road' was a World

War battle trench. The tool-shed and the empty garage behind my house became the cockpit of a fighter plane, a stagecoach, an armoured car, or a tank as our pretend battles were fought and won.

I say, 'our road,' but Julie's house was actually on Elm Tree Avenue, the road one back from ours, with the 'back entry' separating the two rows of terraced houses. This was great because we could call on one another without having to walk all the way to the end of our own streets, turn the corner and then walk a similar distance up to the back door of the other's house. Always the back door, front doors were for strangers, postmen, and 'real visitors' - back doors were for friends and family and never seemed, in my memory, ever to have been locked.

The 'back entry' was a 'safe place to play,' close to home – within Mum's-shouting-distance, no traffic or 'strange men' concerns, somewhere I'm sure our mums and dads – if they ever thought about it - would have preferred us to play, but for Julie and I it also was somewhere that ranked as being as 'dull as dishwater.' The broken tarmac surface was pitted with potholes and loose jagged gravel, the culprit cause of bruises, scrapes, and grazes. Mums with tweezers picking the tiny bits of grit out of knees, palms, and elbows all bore witness to those few times Julie and I had ended up playing football, hide-n-seek, or cricket in the safe confines of 'the back entry.'

Those were the once-a-week bath days – a tin bathtub in front of the coal fire - usually a Saturday night - T-bar leather sandals with small chrome fastening buckles, and the obligatory short grey trousers throughout summer and winter. Dirty necks and snotty noses that left snail trail marks on shirt sleeves and the weekly hair comb-throughs by mothers who seemed to delight in searching for nits.

That last bit was never an enjoyable experience; back then, I had long and very curly straw-coloured hair - where the curls came from and when the fair hair turned from flaxen to a mousey brown, I'll never know, but I do remember that the nit comb was always snagging on tangled bits of my hair and succeeded in tugging more than a few strands out every comb-through.

Boils, blackheads, scabs on elbows and knees, nosebleeds, I guess we were no different from other kids of our age, those living in villages or in the suburbs of towns and cities just after the war had finished, but in my mind, we were something special.

Julie and I were 'The Number One Fun Team,' Batman and Robin, Dan Dare, and his sidekick, whoever that was - Albert, or something like that. Me in a heavy grey cotton three-button shirt, my scruffy patched grey twill shorts, usually held up with bracers or a snake hook buckle elasticated belt - sometimes both. Julie in a 'blow away' cotton school dress. I think her dress would probably have been a pass-me-down from her older sister, who was two years older and who had outgrown the dress, and a yellowy-brown woolly cardie, even in the summer. I think, looking back, Julie's attachment to that old cotton school dress was probably because she thought it made her look older than she actually was. Quite where that thought comes from, I cannot tell. It's just another of those shadowy pictures that comes to mind when searching back through time to those pre-school days.

Being an only child with no brothers or sisters to pester, bully or act as role models and with Julie calling to play with me most every day that summer, needless to say, we formed quite a close informal relationship. The very best of friends!

Chapter 3 - Milk Bottle Games

February 1954 to August 1954

It was our 'milk bottle games' that earned us our notoriety in the area and the place in my memory. According to an aunt who lived close by at the time, it gained us the dubious title of those 'Two Little Sods in Rothesay Avenue.'

I don't know why, but Julie and I thought being a milkman was a pretty cool thing to be. We didn't call it 'cool'; of course, back then, 'being cool' wasn't street talk, but in today-talk, you will get my meaning.

Back in those days the milkman would deliver glass bottles of milk, to the front doorsteps of most houses. The delivery came in crates on an open-sided milk float. I even think the milk float might have been horse-drawn, but my memories of that detail are a bit vague, and I might be mixing things up with the Rag and Bone Man. He definitely did use a horse and cart to do his weekly rounds.

My uncertainty is perhaps understandable as Julie and I were seldom around that early in the morning when the milk deliveries actually took place. Our emergence into the story usually started an hour or so later in the day.

The milkman's rounds started with a drop-off at the infant school, where special crates of milk, each with smaller glass bottles, about one-third of a pint in size, were stacked alongside the school kitchen block. That meant that they were also close to the wire chain-link boundary fence, which enclosed the whole school area, classrooms, offices, and playground.

The fence was meant to serve as a barrier to the outside world, keeping the children and the school property safe and secure, but 'spying trips' made by Julie and me, while defending our make-believe trenches in the adjacent wasteland, showed the fencing was not securely pegged to the ground. So, shielded from sight by a row of hawthorn bushes, it could, with a fair bit of tugging and straining by someone with the incredible strength of Desperate Dan - a hero from the Dandy comic - be pulled and held up, allow his best sidekick to crawl under.

Julie would then grab five or six bottles of milk and pass them through the hole under the fence before crawling back.

The milk wasn't for us to drink; it was a 'prop' we needed for the next phase of our game of 'milkmen.' We secretly delivered the small bottles randomly to those houses nearby where their true milk deliveries were still on their doorsteps waiting to be taken in.

What the recipients of our bonus milk bottles felt we never stopped to ask, but I guess someone soon came to realise it was the 'Two Little Sods' at work and was to add to the reputation that helped earn us our notoriety. This minor larceny couldn't have lasted long, maybe at the most a week or so, and it wasn't every day that we could play our game. Rainy days and weekends were out of the question, of course. Rain kept us in doors, although there wouldn't have been too much rain that summer, and there was no school on weekends - which meant no milk deliveries! But no one, it seemed, bothered to look too closely into what was going on, the school didn't appear to miss the few bottles that went missing, and the people benefiting from the free milk never complained.

However, a divergence in our 'bonus milk deliveries' game metamorphosed into a variation of milk-related larceny.

Taking the cream off the top of the milk was the skulduggery that finally resulted in, I now accept in later years, a well-deserved blemish on our reputations and more than one or two annoyed neighbours.

Chapter 4 - Game Changer

The genuine deliveries of silver aluminium-capped glass bottled pints of milk delivered to the front doorsteps back then were what today would be termed 'regular' milk. The other choice, some people preferred, was sterilised milk, but that was sealed in a hard metal-capped glass bottle and anyway tasted disgusting.

The 'regular milk' was a different matter though, the natural cream in the milk rising to the top of the bottle and settling in the top inch and a half or so, just below the metal foil cap.

In our house, it was my parent's practice to carefully turn the new, unopened bottle upside down and back again to disperse the cream more thoroughly throughout the milk. But left undisturbed, the cream, as both Julie and I were well aware, was the best part of the milk.

Armed with a safety pin, and most kids our age had something held up or held together with a safety pin in those days, we would creep up the garden paths of those houses where the milk still waited on the front doorsteps, puncture a few tiny holes in the middle of the aluminium foil cap and suck out the cream. We would then return the milk bottle back into the crate or onto the doorstep where we had found it. Even at that age, we rationalised that we couldn't steal the cream from the same house every time, so we spread our activities around five or six houses on each of the two closest roads to ours.

Apparently, for a few weeks, I was told by one of my aunts who lived close by, our 'near' neighbours assumed that the small punctures in the aluminium foil milk tops and the cream theft was attributed to hungry blue tits or robins!

I guess at some point we must have been spotted because my Mum sat me down one night to tell me that 'IT HAS TO BLOODY WELL STOP!'

I assume Julie was given the same guidance from her mother because it stopped!

It didn't matter to us greatly because, by then, we had already moved on to other games and adventures.

But, from that point on, though, we seemed to be held responsible for all the minor mischief in the area. Missing dustbin lids (battle shields) and garden canes (swords and lances) were attributed to those 'Two Little Sods in Rothsay Avenue.' Thinking back, we must have both felt at the time it was a bit unfair; there were plenty of other kids of our age in the area up to similar sorts of mischief, but where there was any doubt as to the culprits of whatever happened that summer, it seemed easiest to point the finger of blame at us.

But in truth that didn't really matter, if anything it added to the closeness of our friendship, almost like a badge of honour. For that short time we were a team 'The Two Little Sods', and that closeness lasted all through the Spring and Summer of that year. Still, it must have ended sometime shortly before the new School Term began in September 1954, as neither of us had entered into that next phase of our lives yet.

Early that Autumn, my parents moved house, taking me with them, of course. It must have taken them a bit of time to sort out the relocation, but thinking back, I don't recall I knew anything about the intended move until about the week or so before we actually left Rothesay Avenue and moved to our new house.

Our new house was only a short distance away in Harewood Road but was close to my Granny's house, which meant there was someone living nearby to keep an eye on me when both of my parents were at work. Harewood Road ran up and down a small hillside. Back in those days, the housing to the top half of the hill, where we now lived, was normal two-storey brick-built buildings. Those in the bottom half, however, consisted of the asbestos and metal 'prefabs,' prefabricated houses that were put up as temporary accommodation shortly after the war to ease the housing shortage.

And Harewood Road was where I would live for the next fifteen years of my life. It was where I would soon make new friends, all boys and all of whom, for some reason, came from families living in the prefabricated houses. I think it may have been because most of the younger families, the ones with children of my age, were those that were settled into the temporary housing.

The layout of the prefab estates was such that they encompassed small 'greens' - grass strips about the size of two tennis courts in the middle of the prefab housing blocks, on which we kids could play. No need to play football on the roads, where a tumble would mean grazed knees if you have a 'green' to play on!

I learned new games with my pals; British Bulldog, 'Marlies' with small glass marbles, and 'conkers' with horse chestnuts. I remember we built a trolley from old pram wheels and a thick plank of wood, rescued from the scaffolding materials the builders were using as they built the new housing estate just across the highway close by.

With my new pals, we raced our trolley down the Harewood Road hill with little regard to the dangers we faced of bumped heads, grazed knees and elbows, and bruises all over. And nose bleeds, I mustn't forget nose bleeds, for one reason or another they were a common occurrence back in those days. Everyone seemed to have a crusty blood-stained hanky in their pockets.

We annoyed the folks living in the prefabs with games of Rat-a-tat Ginger - knocking on their front doors and running away. Rat-a-tat Ginger was easy to play on a prefab estate, as there were no front garden paths, fences, or gates to impede our escape. And Hide'n'Seek, with the new gang, became far more fun when there were more than just the two of you playing it.

Just across a field at the bottom of the hill, there was a brook to jump over and float sticks down and even a few ponds in the other fields close by. With frogs, sticklebacks, and newts to capture and keep for a short lifetime in small glass jam jars. So many adventures, distractions, and exciting new games, and there were even some woods nearby on Hersall Common, which my new pals and I could explore and where we could build dens and put up rope swings.

Harewood Road, as I mentioned earlier, wasn't too far away from Rothesay Avenue distance-wise, probably less than half a mile, but it was across the main highway, the A45, and there were also a couple of busy traffic roads between us.

I don't know why we moved house; it was a case of relocating from one end-terrace house with a wooden garage and a small garden to a mid-terrace house with a wooden garage and a small garden. I never asked, and no one ever told me the reason for the move, but what was significant was that it was in a different primary school catchment area, so Julie and I never did get to be starting school together.

The outcome was that we lost contact - my best friend and I had found that fork in the road and gone our separate ways.

Thinking back on it, I recall that I did set out on my own a couple of times in the few months following the house move, returning to Rothesay Avenue and hoping to meet up with Julie again, but it was not to be. I suppose, at that young age, I never planned out my journey very well, and Julie and I lost touch.

In hindsight, I wish I had tried harder, but back then, I had just turned five, and life had moved on. In September of that year, I started at my new school Whoberley Hall Primary, just two roads across from my new house on Harewood Road, and a new chapter in my life had started.

So that was it! Finding Julie would be my new quest.

I would find her and - I don't know - just find her and see how things had turned out for her.

'Another Guinness, Mr. Pepper?' Jason called from behind the bar, my pint was almost drained.

'No thanks,' I replied, 'I have someone I need to find.'

My mind was already racing ahead and beginning to wildly fantasise where things might lead - 'why not Chilli Pepper's Lost and Found Friendly Enquiry Agency?'

I wasn't being serious; just kidding myself. Crazy idea, fuelled by Guinness and an overactive imagination.

'Whoa, slow down there,' I held myself in check. 'Just 'hold your horses on that for a while,' I thought, 'let's just wait and see where the first steps lead.'

I took one last swallow of my beer, wiped the froth off my moustache and beard with the back of my hand, and decided to ease back and 'just go with the flow.'

Chapter 5 - The First Steps

Thursday - November 10th, 2022 am

The next morning I was up and about around 7 am, showered, dressed, fed the dog and cats, breakfasted on a bowl of granola, and let Truffle out into the back garden to sniff out what had happened or not happened overnight. Oh, and of course, after a bit of shouted encouragement from me, to carry out her toilet needs.

I gave Sally a peck on the cheek to say goodbye, she was off to work at the college where she taught. Then I tidied around in the kitchen for a bit, getting one or two of my household jobs done and out of the way.

By around 9:30, I was ready to start giving some serious thought to my new project and was keen to begin my search.

I was determined that this would be a 'fun' project, and it wouldn't do to get too wound up in something that was superficially meant to be just an enjoyable distraction. I figured that if I gave over, say, a couple of hours a day at the most, it should be enough to keep things on an 'even keel' and not disrupt homelife, or marital relationships, too much.

But I was eager to get started; otherwise, I knew I would just keep putting things off, and it would never happen. Now while it was fresh in my mind, I had a 'purpose' and a determination to make something happen.

As chance would have it - not wanting to be the one to let the 'moss grow under my feet' - later that morning, when I was out giving Truffle her proper walk around the village, my project began to take shape.

It was a mild November morning, no rain, but the clouds, forming to the south hinted that we might be in for a shower in the not-too-distant future. Still, I set off on my morning's walk with Truffle, headphones covering my ears, successfully blocking out the outside world as I listened to an Audible story downloaded onto my phone. It was a routine I had come to enjoy whatever the weather, although truth be told it was difficult to get Truffle out in the rain. Still it wasn't raining that morning.

I had one or two different routes which we took, often the weather being a determining factor in the direction we took. Truffle's reluctance to getting wet or walking through sludgy mud was a consideration, and I wasn't too keen on having to wash her paws if she got too mucky either, so we would try to keep as far as possible to the tarred pathways. This morning I chose the route that passed by The Queens Crown pub and down through the adjacent church grounds, and that was where a chance encounter occurred.

St Peters was originally a mediaeval built church, somewhat extended, I read somewhere, in the mid-nineteenth century. A formidable building, one of those types of churches with a square bell tower, complete with battlements and surrounded on all sides by its graveyard.

A pleasant morning route, not too strenuous, relatively mud free, mostly on pavement or tarmac surfaces all the way. We had a different route for evening walks as I didn't relish walking late at night through the graveyard, then along the narrow, unlit path running down from the church. The path leads on to the small bridge which crosses over the shallow river running through our village. Apart from it being unlit, the ivy and some of the tree branches hang down over the pathway at head height. In daylight these can be seen and avoided, but would be a danger to anyone without a torch at night. Also, the pathway is always covered in rotting leaf mulch this time of the year, making it quite a slippery route and, adding to the practical reasons, was that it was bloody spooky to walk that way in the dark.

But in daylight, Truffle and I could avoid the mulch, the overhanging branches, and the ghosts on our walk down by the river. Quite a pleasant route, with the added advantage that I could let Truffle off her lead once we had passed through the graveyard to sniff and pee at her leisure, with just the occasional reminder from me to tell her to get a move on. So this was the route we took this morning.

In the back of my mind, I had already considered that one possible source of information on people living within an area might be through church records. And, as luck would have it, as we walked by the door to the church, we passed by a tall, middle-aged gentleman in a rather scruffy faded grey/green boiler suit, who appeared to be busying himself tidying up the entrance way of the church with a broom.

'Nothing to lose,' I thought, 'this guy could be a source of information, someone connected with the church who might possibly be able to give me a pointer as to how I could begin to make a start with my search.'

I was well aware that there would be no record of Julie in the archives of St Peters; what I was looking for was something of a more general nature - some sort of direction as to what I should be looking for in the church records and how accessible they might be.

'Hello there,' I called over, 'excuse me, but I was wondering if you might be able to give me a bit of advice?'

The man smiled and stopped brushing the entrance way and leaned on his broom to give me his attention.

'Lovely little dog,' he said, reaching down to stroke her and scratch her ear. 'What sort is he?'

'She,' I corrected him, 'is a Dorkie.' Explaining that Truffle was of mixed lineage 'Dachshund and a Yorkie,' and adding, 'best of both breeds.'

By then, my little aid had rolled over onto her back to get her tummy scratched.

I went on to claim that I was an amateur writer and that I was thinking of writing a story which, although not strictly true, saved me from having to give 'chapter and verse' as to why I found it necessary to be searching for someone I had known, and then lost contact with, over 70 years ago.

As first steps go, it was a start, albeit a small start, but still a step forwards on my investigative journey. The man, it turned out, was a church official of some sort. He wasn't wearing a clerical collar under his boiler suit, that I could see, but perhaps that was normal. Maybe vicars only wore their collars for official religious activities, not when they are pushing a broom around the church entrance. I didn't enquire as to what his role actually was, so perhaps a curate? Not being a regular church goer - more a weddings and funeral visitor, I had unsurprisingly never crossed paths with this gentleman before. But whatever his role was, he seemed pleasant enough.

'Happy to help if I'm able to,' he offered.

I briefly told him of my search for someone I had previously known quite some considerable time back.

'It's not someone from the parish here,' I explained. 'The person I am searching for lived in Coventry seventy years back, and her house would have been in the diocese of St James Church in Tile Hill.'

St James Church was the closest church to where Julie and I used to live, a short walk from both Rothesay and Elm Tree Avenues.

'I'd be happy to help if I can, but from what you've said, trying to locate someone from seventy years back,' a broad smile on his face. 'that will be quite a challenge; I wouldn't think you'll find it an easy journey. But best of luck. You could start, I suppose,' he added, 'by going on-line and looking in 3BMD.'

I thanked him, making a mental note of '3BMD'; no idea what it meant and hadn't had the sense to ask the guy when I had the chance. But it kept my thoughts racing as I finished my walk with Truffle.

As it turned out, however, once I had begun searching through Google for '3BMD', I found that it was actually 'Free BMD' that I should have been searching for. 'Getting your hearings muddled up with your earrings,' as my mother would have said!

Still, no time was lost, and my search had officially begun. Free Births, Marriages, and Deaths, an online record of all such events that were registered through church authorities.

My initial search online knocked me back a few steps, I had obviously not carried out the search properly as it seemed that there were upwards of four thousand Julie Bishops registered in Coventry in 1950 - even I figured that couldn't be right - I had screwed it up somehow. But I was a novice at this and determined to try again later.

I thought it best to try an alternative approach first. This time I tried an 'online' search through BNA - British Newspaper Articles - for birth announcements - in the Coventry Evening Telegraph between September 1949 and September 1950. This would, I figured, have covered Julie's possible birth dates and might then lead to some other link identifying her family's current whereabouts. BNA identified 20 instances where someone with the name Julie Bishop had been mentioned in articles within that time frame, not really leading me directly anywhere, but at least the numbers seemed more plausible. Still, I wasn't comfortable with the approach I was taking or confident that it was moving me in the right direction or closer towards finding the pertinent information needed to locate Julie.

I came to realise that I needed some help with this! Beyond basic word processing skills, I had to accept that computer technology and search engines, or whatever, were all a bit beyond my comprehension. If this was the future of detective work, maybe my prospects of becoming a Private Enquiry Agent were a trifle ambitious.

Quite apart from that there came the realisation that the only name that I could rely upon being consistent was 'Julie', her Christian name, and that was absolutely useless when it came to trying to find someone after seventy-odd years.

The elusive Ms. Bishop would, in all likelihood, have, at some time in her life, got married and almost certainly would then have taken the surname of her husband. So it wasn't even sensible to think I could reliably trace someone who still bore the name Julie Bishop.

Despondent I might have been - but I was not prepared to give up at the first hurdle. Surrendering without making a token effort was not an acceptable outcome. I needed to think it through logically, employ some of my problem-solving skills and possibly go back to the beginning. Take a step back to the source of where it all started. Visit the playgrounds where Julie and I had, all of those years back, formed our friendship.

Chapter 6 - A Backwards Step

I have lived in many different places both in the UK and overseas throughout my life; however, where Sal and I are living now is less than thirty miles away from the playgrounds of my youth. Coventry is a short drive from our village, and Harewood Road and Rothesay Avenue, for that matter, are only around 30 to 45 minutes' drive away. So, I theorised that a visit back to the place where my pre-school memories and escapades had taken place was a prerequisite for my current little adventure, an unavoidable requirement if I was going to do things properly.

This time though, instead of just rushing in head-first, my usual approach to new challenges, I planned my return visit to the scene of my early childhood with a little more care.

I decided to journey to Rothesay Avenue first and take a look, from the outside, at the house where I had been born and had spent those pre-school years. Perhaps walk through the 'back entry' to see if that might ring a few bells. Maybe speak with a few of the current residents I might meet and discover if I could pick up any leads from them. I also planned a visit to St James church up on Tile Hill Lane, maybe. At last, I would be doing something practical and actively looking for clues instead of just staring at a computer screen.

I also decided that it would be a good idea to take Truffle (aka Wolf) with me. This wasn't just a flight of fancy; it was a part of my planned approach. My logic here being that if any of the local residents I came across felt concerned about a stranger walking around their 'back entry' or anywhere in the area to the rear of their houses, the presence of a small, cute dog on a pink retractable lead would lessen their discomfort.

A stroke of genius? Well, maybe not, but having tried it, I can, in retrospect, vouch for the fact that it works, at least to some small degree.

So, five days after our trip by the village church, Truffle and I set off for Coventry. It was mid-November, and, as I had said earlier, the weather was dull and cold, but the threat of rain looked to have gone away. This aligned itself with the breakfast television weather-forecast on the morning news channel, so no reason for delaying my investigation any further.

First taking Truffle for a short walk around by the library, just across the road from our house, to allow her to address her toiletry needs and catch up on any new smells that had occurred overnight. I then attached her, in her car harness, to the safety belt on the back seat of my car and climbed into the driving seat. I started the engine, and the car radio automatically tuned itself into some channel Sally had programmed in when she had used my car last. It was one of the music channels, and it came on mid-way through playing the Rolling Stones classic – 'I can't get no – Satisfaction.' Again I had to trust that the words to the song were not a bad omen – as I set off for Coventry.

It was about 10 am, and the traffic was relatively light just a few delivery vans with the odd lorry mixed in, here and there, and a handful of cars travelling along the A46. At that time of day, the sparsity of traffic was of no great surprise, given that most people with cars would probably have already travelled to work.

The whole journey took no more than forty minutes. I turned off the A46 at the traffic lights leading up Tile Hill Lane, just past an old theatre building that many years ago had once been the Standard Cinema. Another relic of long-ago memories, the first cinema I had ever been to, probably back then with my dad, to watch Cowboys and Indians films with stars like John Wayne, Gary Cooper and James Stuart.

At the first turning on the right, I turned off and drove past the top end of Rothesay Avenue and down the next right-hand turning, into Julie's road Elm Tree Avenue. I had chosen to take this route for no particular reason other than it just seemed an easy way to access Rothesay Avenue from the lower end of the road. It led onto where the old primary school and the waste land where our playtime battle trenches had once been and most of our adventures had taken place. Now the school and the patch of grassland has been replaced by two rows of terraced houses. Sentiment aside, choosing this approach also meant my car would be facing in the right direction to lead to Saint James Church, where I planned to go next.

One of those odd things, that stuck out in my mind as something different from my memories of times back then, was that the front gardens of almost all the houses in Rothesay Avenue had now been sacrificed so as to turn them into paved, or pebbled, parking driveways. Some of the houses also had cars parked in front of them. I guess that after normal work time, between 7 am and 6 pm, the drives would be full, and the road undoubtedly crowded with parked cars, two wheels on the road and two on the pavement. This a small reflection of how times had changed and how the number of motor cars on the roads today had far exceeded the thinking of the street planning authorities of the 1940s.

It was messy, but at least at this time of the day, it allowed sufficient room for my car to drive up the road without too much trouble.

In my memories, the road had seemed much wider in my childhood days, and there were certainly far fewer cars about. Back then, the older kids used the road as a football pitch. Two coats thrown down about eight feet apart were the goal, and the paths on either side were the side-lines. Not so now. Even at this time of the day, there were too many parked cars, which left a parking challenge for me.

Still, as chance would have it, I was able to find a space almost directly out front of my old house. I don't know why, but it felt good to see that the current owners had not been one of those to sacrifice their front garden for a parking lot. Just as in my memory, there was still a privet hedge and a wooden front garden gate. It couldn't have been the same hedge; Google later told me that privet hedges live for around forty years, so later house owners must have decided at some time in the past to replace it.

Surreptitiously, I took a few photographs of the house with my iPhone. I wasn't quite sure of how that might actually help things, but Sally had suggested that it might be useful, and I knew better than to pass-by on any sensible suggestion that I might later come to regret.

I unclipped the safety harness holding Truffle to the seatbelt in the back of my car, scooped her out and attached her lead, then off we walked up the road, stopping - of course - at nearly every garden gate and lamppost to allow her the sniffing bonanza of a new territory. It also allowed me time to take a furtive look at the houses and what little could be observed in the spaces between them, of the gardens and 'back entry' beyond.

One significant thing I did notice was that the two or three alleyway entrances to the 'back entry' had been fenced off with high and padlocked metal bar gates. Some sort of security safeguard, I suppose. So any thoughts of being able to walk up the back entry and revisiting any memories from that direction were blown away. Still, the cursory peeks I did manage to get through the gated alleyways did point towards it having stayed true to my memories of the area.

As we walked, I noticed, on the pavement, the traces of partly erased chalked numbers set out in a grid form. The remnants of a children's game of hopscotch - a flashback to those days when Julie and I had played that same game, perhaps on those or similar paving slabs close by. Seventy years on, and it made me smile that there were children living in this neighbourhood who were still playing some of the same games as we had all those years ago.

I walked the length of the road, taking in as much as I could of what little there was to learn to aid my research.

Near the top end of the road, an older gentleman around my age was tidying some flowerpots in his front paved driveway, and as we approached, he stopped to smile down at my cute little dog. Truffle, as if on cue, pulled towards him, tail wagging like crazy, as she tends to do with everyone, to get stroked. A trait which, as planned, again worked well for me, acting as a 'curtain breaker' and conversation starter.

I gave the man a friendly smile, and we chatted, for a few minutes, about Truffle - 'what a lovely little dog she was' and all of that stuff. Truffle played her part, jumping up at the gentleman's gate so he could reach over and ruffle her ears.

I explained that I had once lived on this street a long-long time ago, in the early 1950's and was just looking to see what, if anything, had changed over the years.

'Oh, my wife and I only moved into the area around ten years back, but little has changed since we moved in. We really like it here; the neighbours are a friendly bunch, and we have street parties whenever there is a reason for doing so. Nice that. Never used to do that sort of thing where we used to live.'

'Much has changed.' I reflected. 'I see that they have built some new houses at the bottom there, where the waste land used to be and the old primary school has gone now.'

'Yes, things change.' He hesitated for a second or two, then, 'They will have changed quite a bit from when you lived here, I suppose.'

We both smiled at one another and talked about how things had changed in life, like old folks do. Some things for the better and some for the worse. Most of our conversation rambled on and on for some time about changes in the neighbourhood, again some good, some not so good. One thing he did recall was that, from conversations he had had with his neighbours back when he first moved in, he'd learned that there had once been a piece of wasteland to the rear of his house. But years before, the land there had been reclaimed and incorporated into the adjoining gardens.

This small bit of recollection of his unlocked a part-memory of my own. There it was, I recalled. There had indeed been a small area of wasteland behind the houses at the top end of the road between Rothesay and Elm Tree Avenues, I had forgotten all about that. Julie and I had sometimes played there, it was where our 'Den' had been. Between the two streets and towards the top end of the 'back entry', a small area of unkempt grassland where there had been an old, half-buried, corrugated metal and turf air-raid shelter. Our 'Den', well not just Julie's and mine, I suppose all of the other kids in the surrounding area also called that old air-raid shelter their 'Den'. There had also been a large, blackened patch of burnt earth there, if my memory serves me right, where some of the older kids had once built their bonfires on November 5th. I don't actually recall ever going to see the bonfire there, I suppose my parents would have thought me too young, as a four-year-old, to go along on my own in the dark to see the firework display. A nicely awakened memory, but no closer in my search to find Julie.

Truffle and I walked our return journey back to my car, again revisiting every lamppost and wall corner on route to allow her to sniff and mark her presence, before we set off to drive to our next point of research, St James's Church, back on Tile Hill Lane.

Chapter 7 – On the Trail

Monday - November 21st, 2022, 12:30 pm

St James's is the local Church of England (C of E) church on Tile Hill Lane, no more than a three or four minute walk away from the top end of Rothesay Avenue.

Quite a formidable building with its traditional pointed roof and small bell tower. Apparently built just before the Second World War, it was where I, and most of the other children in the area, would have been baptised.

My assumption was that if Julie was C of E, she would also have been baptised there, and if she and her parents had remained in Elm Tree Avenue, Julie may well also have been married there. Well, it was a possibility - wasn't it? Certainly, something worth following up on.

Across the road from the church was The Newlands pub set back behind a sizeable car park, and that is where I pulled my car into.

The car park was surprisingly quite full of cars for lunchtime. Looking at the advertisement on display in one of the pub windows, I surmised that the reason for the lunch-time parking was either the 'Speciality Brunch' - a full English Breakfast - on offer, or - like me, because people just found it a useful place for parking when using the small shopping area just across the way, leading up to, but on the same side of the road as the church.

I unfastened Truffle's car harness, reattached her lead and gathered up my notebook - another sensible suggestion from Sally, something to take notes in as I went along - and the two of us, me and Truffle that is - walked across to the church.

I had that uncomfortable feeling of being watched. Subconsciously, I rationalised it was probably someone looking out from the pub, annoyed that I was guilty of using their car park while not calling in to give them my custom. In their position, I guess I would have felt the same.

Still best to ignore it, assume an 'air of innocence' and not look back in the direction of the pub windows.

Just a man walking his cute little dog! (a stroke of genius)

The three large wooden front doors to the church were closed and locked, something I hadn't expected. For some obtuse reason, I had assumed that church doors were always open for possible passing worshipers to just call in at any time. I guess that it was a sign of the times - lock your doors or risk losing your church belongings. I was a little disappointed as I had hoped to be able to take a peek into the church aisles; after all, not only was it where I had been christened, it was also where in later years, I had, as a nine-year-old Senior Sixer, with the 80th Cub Scouts, paraded on special occasions like Poppy Day.

Re-stoking memories again. Well, why not? That was what this was all about, wasn't it?

Anyway, the front doors were locked, and that was that. I walked Truffle around the left-hand side of the church to see if there were any other doors or points of access, there weren't. To the right of the church, however, there was a gate leading to a detached house. Access to the gate and the front garden of the house was shared with the front gates of the church. The connection was fairly obvious, the house had to have some sort of relationship with the church itself. Could this be my detection skills coming into play once more? Well, probably nothing to write home about; as I mentioned before, it was pretty clear that there was some sort of a connection.

Making my way down the small path towards the front door, I spotted a man looking out of the front patio window of the house from where he was sitting at his desk, and he also noticed he had a visitor, me.

By the time I arrived at his front door, it was opening, and he was smiling at me before bending down to scratch Truffle behind her ear. He was, I would guess, in his mid to late fifties and dressed in pretty 'relax at home' casual clothing - loose tartan shirt, baggy brown corduroy trousers

– worn for comfort, I surmised, not style - and of course carpet slippers.

'Good morning'. I said, again, not actually aware of whether it was still morning or not.

'Good afternoon.' he smiled back at me, putting me straight. 'Can I help you?' With a strong Birmingham accent, there was little doubt as to where this gentleman originated from.

'Sorry to intrude,' I said, returning his smile, 'but are you connected with the church in any way?'

It might have been obvious, but it would have been wrong to have made any assumptions without politely asking, and anyway, it was an opening to let him clarify what his connection to the church might be.

'Yes', he said, 'I am the Vicar - what a cute little dog, what's his name?'

I noticed that he was also not wearing his clerical collar, so I figured I had an answer to what I had been wondering about when I met the other clerical official at our village church.

'She is Truffle', I told him, 'Aka Wolf'. I had recently started to throw in the last bit - the Wolf bit - more frequently; it generally worked in helping to break the ice and raise a smile.

Truffle played her part well, wagging her tail vigorously and gyrating about - like the good 'stage-prop' she was - as the vicar continued to scratch her behind her ear.

'How can I help?'

'I'm researching some local history', I told him, 'For a book I am looking to write. A novel.'

Using the explanation I had used before and without it being too far from the truth, especially as I am now recording my encounter in this journal.

I explained to the Vicar that I had spent some of my early years living in this area, during which time I had made a close friend with someone with whom I had since lost contact.

I think it may have aroused his interest a little as he seemed happy to chat with me about the few approaches I had taken so far and to explain to me how church records on Births, Deaths and Marriages were currently maintained.

When, early in our doorstep chat, I explained that my contact with Julie had been lost about seventy years ago, I sensed it triggered in him a look of some regret.

Church records, he explained, were only kept in the church archives for up to six years, then apparently, it was a requirement that they were to be passed through to the relevant Government Records office.

He looked down as if to be giving the whole matter some thought, then told me that he did, however, have some of his parishioners with longer memories, and undertook to speak with one particular couple who, in their late seventies, he thought might be able to recall that far back.

Inwardly I doubted they would be of any help in that regard, as being in their late seventies would have meant that, as children, they would have been some years older than Julie and I back then, and would, in all likelihood, have shown little interest in the antics of a couple of younger kids. The age difference is an important factor when you are growing up; being one year older or younger meant you are in a different social group to those other children who are a little older or younger than you. Still, whatever, I wasn't about to leave any stones unturned; if he could uncover any leads, great! If not - well, nothing lost!

I gave the vicar my telephone number, and he promised to give me a call if he had anything to tell me after having spoken with the couple he was thinking of.

We said our goodbyes - a nice guy, I thought - as I walked Truffle back to my car - but a bit of a blind alley.

There was definitely a feeling of those 'pub eyes' on me again, but glancing around surreptitiously, I couldn't make out anyone looking my way. Just my 'guilty parking' conscience, I guess. I was getting paranoid! Still, I took care not to look in the direction of the pub's front windows and played the caring dog owner, focusing my attention on Truffle as I got into my car and drove away.

Chapter 8 - A Different Approach

Between 22nd and 26th November 2022

I was beginning to feel a mite despondent, I seemed to be getting nowhere, it felt like an impossible journey. I was looking for someone who had been my closest friend for no longer than six months, seventy or so years ago. Not only that, but I also didn't know what her current surname was, I didn't know where she lived now, nor for that matter, whether she was still alive. After all the list of friends and acquaintances I had known, who had passed away in recent years, was lengthening rapidly – I wasn't getting any younger.

My dalliance with Google searches on Free BDM hadn't proved very successful, and I was now beginning to realise that this was because I had been searching for the wrong person. What I needed to do was to start again, this time search for someone, a male relative of Julie's, whose surname was still Bishop, then see if I could, convince that person to tell me where Julie lived now, or at least what her married name was. Maybe even, if luck was on my side, get him to put me in touch with her.

The old-fashioned telephone directories that you used to find in the red street-side public telephone boxes were, I surmised, something of the past. Like the telephone boxes themselves, they had had their day, and that meant I was left trying to find my way on the internet. But, once I began searching I found it proved much easier than I had imagined. My Google search led me to a website called '192.com free'. This was a publicly available version of the Electoral Roll, which provided the names and addresses of UK residents over the age of 18. There were several similar 'search engine' sites all refining the search information; however, these all seemed to require a fee or the purchase of 'credits,' and for my little 'fun project' exercise, I wasn't, at this point in my enquiry anyway, prepared to spend money needlessly.

So I played around with '192.com free' for an hour or so and identified more or less 100 people with the surname Bishop living in the CV5 Coventry postcode area and included some of the neighbouring towns and villages. I narrowed the search down as far as I could, trying to minimise the variables to a manageable level by focusing on the Tile Hill area of Coventry, and gradually widened my search until I had a short list of those living in the relatively close proximity of Rothesay Avenue.

This left me with a manageable list of 15 plausible possibilities, my intent being to contact each in turn and ask if they had an aunt, or relative, who was in their early seventies called Julie and whose maiden name would have been Bishop. Not a simple task as I couldn't just turn up 'cold' on someone's doorstep, even with a cute little dog tucked under my arm and start asking about someone's Auntie or Granny Julie.

This time I would have to put my trust in several well-rehearsed phone calls and a bit of verbal reasoning. I won't give away my technique in this area (a) because it worked and I might need to use it again in the future. And (b) because I'm not sure of the legality, nor am I particularly proud of my technique in having stretch the truth to people in such a way so as to gather the information I was looking for. In my defence, I can console myself with the rationale that my reasons for using a fabricated background story as a means of acquiring this information were entirely altruistic. Anyway, that's my story, and I'm sticking to it.

At last, luck seemed to be falling my way. What I found from my third call was that the gentleman I spoke with actually did have an Aunty Julie who lived in Kenilworth, the small town close by, with its famous ruined castle. The town was located about halfway between the village where I lived and Coventry. This Julie's married surname was Saltmarsh, but he was pretty sure he recalled that, before her marriage to her late husband, she had lived in Coventry and - a bonus - that her maiden name had definitely been Bishop.

I was on to something at last!

After a little coaxing and reassurance from me that I was immensely grateful, I would not be bothering her at all, and promising him that his aunt, Mrs. Saltmarsh, would be thrilled and eternally grateful to him for passing me her phone number (I probably laid it on a 'bit thick'), he gave me her telephone phone number.

I thought I had been cleverer than I actually was, but this - I didn't know at the time - was not the case.

However, at last, I had something to work with!!!

I made Sally and myself a coffee, decaf - no biscuits - Sally was minding her diet, watching what she was eating, which meant - by default, I was also minding my diet - and brought her 'up to speed' with what I had managed to find out so far. I was pretty psyched up about the whole thing, full of how clever and resourceful I had been, a real 'true-to-life' private eye in the making.

I didn't somehow, however, get the feeling that Sally was quite so confident or assured of my abilities, but that didn't matter; at last, the ball was rolling.

'You need to think things through carefully before you go ringing this lady up out of the blue. Think through where you want the conversation to go. Don't go expecting that she will even remember you, even if she is the right person you have been searching for. Also, even if she is, she may not have the same happy reflexions of the times back when you were pals. Don't expect too much more than just an 'hello.' Just because your memory of your childhood exploits, back seventy years ago, were good and are now somewhat refreshed from your recent research, doesn't mean she will remember, or see, things the same.' I was told.

'Remember, this was supposed to just be a bit of fun. A distraction from just sitting at home watching the tele all day or doing Wordle on your phone.' Sally reminded me.

'Don't get carried away with things, you're supposed to be retired, and I can find plenty of things for you to do if you get bored.'

This coming from the woman who had told me to 'Get out and make some friends' and that I was 'in danger of becoming an 'old man.'

I didn't bother to argue my point; there was nothing to be gained from making waves, and, in essence, she was right of course, but having taken the inquiry so far, it would have made the whole investigation pointless not to close the loop. Sal was okay with this, again just reminding me to, in her words, 'keep it light.'

Chapter 9 – Coffee with a Friend

I waited until mid-morning the following day, before making my call. That old nervousness tumbling in my guts, I wasn't sure whether or not I wanted someone to pick up at the other end. Well, I did, I suppose, but l was just quite 'on edge' about the whole thing.

'Hi, could I speak with Mrs. Saltmarsh, please?'

'Yes, speaking.'

'Good morning, my name is John Pepper; I think we may have met some years back when you were still called Julie Bishop.'

There was something of a delay before she spoke again.

'I don't recall you. When was this supposed to be?'

She probably thought this was another of those annoying scam calls that seem to be on the increase nowadays.

'Well, it was quite a long time ago, we used to play together in the days before, well before we both first started school.' I threw in before she could hang up.

Again, the line went quiet for what seemed to be a long five to ten seconds, then.

'John Pepper….. John Pepper? ….. Chilli Pepper? …. Is that Chilli Pepper? …..Oh my God….., Oh my God….., the rat boy!'

I had found Julie!

Not only that, but she also remembered me and, although somewhat taken aback, actually sounded - if I was interpreting her reaction correctly - quite pleasantly surprised to hear from me.

My nervousness and trepidation went straight 'out of the window.' We chatted and laughed together for a few minutes about nothing of any importance, shooting half-remembered names of other kids at one another. I couldn't hide the smile on my face, and I'm sure it came across in my voice. I told her where I was living now, not far from Kenilworth, and how it would be nice to meet up with her again.

'Do you know Kenilworth at all?' She asked. 'There are quite a few nice coffee places here where we could meet.'

'I'm afraid I don't know the area too well at all. I've driven through it a few times and visited the Castle once or twice, but I never really had too much of a reason beyond that for getting to know the place all that well.'

'Well there is the 'Forest Coffee House,' the coffee is excellent, it's in the centre of the town, and there is a car park not too far away. It's got signposts up to the parking area, so easy to get to. I'm free tomorrow morning, Friday. Is that not too soon? Love to meet you again. Is that okay with you? Do you know where it is?'

I hardly had time to catch my breath - crikey, this lady could talk quickly. I paused briefly while I did a quick mental review of what was on my calendar for tomorrow. I was pretty certain it was clear.

'Nope,' I told her, 'But don't worry - tomorrow's fine, and I'll find it. Shall we say around 10 am?'

After all, here we were, both in our seventies and retired from work, so our time was pretty much our own - well, more or less - there were still lawns to mow, doors, walls, and gates to paint, cats to feed and cute little dogs to walk.

'Tomorrow it is then, 10 am - can't wait to catch up again after what, it must be over seventy years.' It sounded as if she giggled that last bit.

-0-0-0-

Still, the next day, I was 'up and about'; the weather was holding dry, just the occasional glimmer of the sun shining through an almost total blanket of light grey clouds. It was early, even for me, around seven in the morning, but there I was out giving Truffle her constitutional morning walk around local church grounds. Around six thousand steps or so, according to my Fitbit watch. A relatively short walk, but taking nearly an hour to complete as my small and persistent little companion insisted we fully inspect every lamppost and 'sniffing point' on our journey.

Then, tidying up my appearance a bit before setting out and armed with my notebook and pencil, I gave Sally a hug, and off I drove to Kenilworth, about a thirty-minute drive away from where I lived.

The traffic was light in the town, not too surprising given it was mid-morning and most people would have been wherever it was they were supposed to be at that time of day. I drove along the main street, the High Street, running through the centre of the small shopping area. There didn't appear to be too many people out shopping or walking around. Just a normal weekday morning, I suppose, with most people at work or school and the miserable weather deterring all but the most ardent recreational shoppers.

The 'Forest Coffee House' was located on the main road at the corner of the town square. It wasn't far from the historic castle ruins, but far enough away to lose out on any of the associated charms. Still, this was to be just somewhere for our initial meeting, and if there ever were any subsequent get-togethers following this, we could always find somewhere more suited to our needs.

Even though Julie had assured me that it would be easy to locate, it was still a bit of a sod trying to find my way to the parking area at the short-stay car park. But eventually, I found a slip road leading me in, paid RingGo for a two-hour stay, and made my way to the 'Forest Coffee House.'

I was running about ten minutes ahead of our agreed 'meet up' time and, as it was something of a cold and damp morning, I was pretty well wrapped up in my padded winter coat. Canvas backpack, with my laptop in it, slung loosely over one shoulder, and my black beanie hat on my head, pulled down to keep my ears warm, I figured I would be probably difficult to make out - for anyone 'keeping an eye out' for me - or so I thought. I was wrong! No more than a second or two after making my entry into the cafe, a smartly dressed lady in a plaid woollen coat and wearing a dark green beret was standing up at one of the tables near the window, a broad smile on her face and waving her arms wildly about whilst grinning in my direction. This had to be Julie, I surmised. It was.

'Hello! Chilli?' she shouted in a high-pitched smiley way, that I was sure was not her normal voice. Guaranteed to make everyone else in the cafe turn to look at me. So much for decorum or a quiet entry.

Her eyes were bright with delight, and I sensed barely concealed humour, and I immediately warmed to her for recognising me, albeit I surely couldn't have looked anything like I did when she had once known me.

'That's me…….. Julie, I guess?' I smiled back.

Some smart detective I was. I held out my hand to shake hers; she lifted her hand as if to shake mine, then raised it up beside her head and said, 'How Kemosabe!'

That she had called me 'Kemosabe' told me a great deal. It confirmed that she was indeed 'my Julie', the friend I had known so many years ago, in a different life, or so it seemed. It told me that she had a sound memory of the friendship we forged seventy-odd years ago that might still survive, and it told me she had retained a great sense of humour.

'Julie, you can't know how happy it makes me feel to hear you call me Kemosabe again after all those years.' And, joking aside, I really meant it.

'You wouldn't be so happy,' she smirked, 'if you knew what Kemosabe meant.'

Okay, that was one up to her. The old ones are the best! Jokes, I mean - not the old fogies like Julie and me.

Lots of smiling at one another leading up to a big hug - careful to avoid the black framed reading glasses hanging from a bright red cord strung around her neck - to mark our seventy-year reunion. I don't know which of us grabbed the other first, it didn't really matter, the warmth of the reunion was there, and we clung together for what seemed a long five or ten seconds.

'Gosh, you haven't changed at all,' she said. 'All that white stuff on your chin and top lip, you look just like you did when you used to bury your face in your ice cream cone.'

'That happens to be an extremely fashionable and neatly trimmed moustache and beard you are talking about, and I'm told by those who truly know me that the shade of grey of my facial hair quite suits me. You should grow one.'

'Shades of Grey, hey!'

Greetings over; we sat down opposite one another, still smiling like a couple of school kids. I don't know what came over me, but I reached across and took her hand in mine, and we both sat together for a short while, staring at one another. Julie's head was just gently shaking from side to side as if in disbelief. Time had been kind to her, and she had, I could see, taken care of her appearance and fitness over the years, and I couldn't help but think she was one smart lady.

There was a half-empty cup of coffee on the table in front of her on my arrival, so she had been here in the Forest Coffee House quite some time ahead of our prearranged meet-up time. She had used her time to secure a table for us, which was fortunate as the seating spaces and, indeed, floor space seemed to be filling up quite rapidly.

The coffee shop looked like it was a favourite meeting place for young mothers with their prams and pushchairs, all parked alongside the tables, so there was plenty of residual background noise competing with Michael Bublé on the sound system singing about 'Santa Claus Coming To Town.' I excused myself for a brief minute and made my way up to the counter to order a black Americano and two almond croissants, my favourites - one of which I must add, on returning to our table, I graciously passed over to Julie.

'Thank heavens for that,' she giggled, 'I thought you were back being Mr. Piggy again like you always were in the old days.' Her normal voice was quite deep and throaty in a rather warm and engaging way.

'I think you must be thinking of someone else,' I countered. 'Age, it is sadly apparent, has befuddled your mind.' And we were there. It was just like the seventy years of separation in our friendship had never happened. We were back in the closeness of the days of the 'Two Little Sods' once again.

We both continued to study each other as we settled back to enjoy our coffee and begin the process of re-establishing our relationship.

I wet my index finger with my tongue and used the tip of the finger to mop up the crisp croissant flakes that had fallen onto my plate. Then had to shield away a smile behind my hand as I noticed Julie was doing exactly the same finger-mopping procedure with her croissant.

What her true impression of me was, I'll never know, but Julie was a fine and intelligent-looking woman. She hadn't tried to hide her age with hair colouring or more than the slightest application of make-up, but her short, neatly trimmed grey hairstyle suited her well, emphasising the natural strong but attractive contours of her face.

We chatted for well over our allotted and intended couple of hours. So, I used my phone app for RingGo to extend my parking stay for a further hour. We took turns to recall memories of that short spell of time when we played together - so - so very long ago.

'So what made you decide to try to find me again after so long?'

'Just a silly whim, really. I needed something to get me out of the dormant apathy I was beginning to sink into. My wife told me to find some new friends, but I thought it might be more fun to find my oldest friend - and that's you!'

'Charming, I'm old, but not so old,' she said, feigning a look of annoyance.

I smiled and explained how it came about that I was looking to find her after so many years, the route I had taken, what worked and what didn't in my search, and how, in the end, it had turned out to be a relatively simple process.

She was 'spellbound,' amazed that I had taken the time to search and had stuck with it until eventually finding her, and I think, secretly, she was quite thrilled that she had featured so highly in my childhood memories.

We both topped up with a second cup of coffee, the caffeine intake no doubt boosting the exuberance at our reunion after so many years.

Julie could remember a whole tranche of details about the things we had done, the games we had played, and the other kids we had played with, and as she spoke, she rekindled once again those forgotten memories for me. Her recollection of detail seemed to be considerably better than mine. Probably it's something of a gender age thing because I quite often find the same seems to apply at home with Sally. Although I will, with caution, add that sometimes in my case, 'selective memory loss' does come into play.

Our recollections rambled on, triggering new partial memories in each other until, beginning to feel a few hunger pangs arising, I went back up to the counter and ordered a couple of paninis, thereby extending our morning coffee into an early lunch as well.

We skipped through our life stories, exchanging details of our partners - my wife, who had encouraged and supported my search for Julie and Julie's husband, a retired 'very senior' Senior Police Officer who had sadly passed away two years prior, one of the early COVID casualties. We bragged about our children, grandchildren, and pets and skipped through the careers we had enjoyed before retirement.

It turned out that, like her husband, Julie had spent most of her working life in the West Midlands Police Force, for the later years fulfilling a role as a LIO (Local Intelligence Officer), which meant nothing to me, but she explained 'It involves the gathering and analysis of the information needed in the investigation and resolution of criminal activities. Basically, all the hard work needed to bring the buggers to court.'

'After retiring from the police, I kicked up dust for a few years, missed the old work routine and the interesting mix of people, I guess. Tom, my husband, had retired a couple of years earlier, so there we both were with plenty of time on our hands. Felt a bit like flotsam washed up on a beach – no longer a valuable resource for anyone.'

She looked away, probably thinking back to her time as a serving police officer.

'But that changed when we were both contacted by an old friend in the NCA - the National Crime Agency - and asked if we would be prepared to pick up some work as NCA Specials – we were told we were too valuable to let go,' she said jokingly, but not hiding too well the pride she obviously felt.

'It's just part-time, usually one, or at the most two days a week and all volunteer work, but it keeps the old brain ticking,' a broad smile lighting her face.

I grinned back, silently thinking, 'Sounds like there could be more than just a grain of truth in that.'

She brushed over some of the sorts of things she became involved in, 'But mainly, it's all office work,' she said. I felt she was somewhat underplaying the role she actually held. Seemed, from what Julie was saying, that a lot of her focus was on investigating drug trafficking.

'The 'County Lines' problem, with youngsters and vulnerable people being used as drug runners moving drugs and money across police and county boundaries.' She told me.

I must admit I didn't have much of a clue as to what 'County Lines' entailed, but it all sounded extremely interesting, and I was impressed by some of the activities she told me she had been actively engaged in.

It sounded so much more interesting and exciting than my work life had been. All those years, I'd spent drawing Gantt charts, spreadsheets, and multi-project modelling in a series of 'process improvement' management roles. The 'Mumbo jumbo' of it all seemed to tie others up, but it always seemed relatively logical and straight forward to me.

However, on reflection and in truth, I truly enjoyed my pre-retirement work. As jobs go, it didn't give me the excitement that it sounded like Julie's job created, but it did provide me with a fair amount of freedom to work through problems and be involved in the implementation of the final outcome. A job which, for me, simply meant taking a fresh look at how 'things' were currently being done - by people whose initial response to my intervention always seemed to start with the phrase 'We've always done it this way' and helping them to find - for themselves - smarter ways of doing those 'things.'

It also - and that was the best bit - allowed me to travel to a host of different countries all around the world, all expenses paid, to places I would never have normally had the opportunity to visit.

'In truth,' Julie told me, 'I really miss my time with the regular Police, but one of my sons - I have two sons, Ben and Mikey – Ben is still working as a West Midlands police officer. He is a Detective Sergeant,' she announced proudly, 'and he keeps me up to date on all the happenings back there.'

Her time with the NCA had also allowed her to keep herself involved in law enforcement and gave her the confidence that she still had a role to play and remained a contributing asset.

Thinking back, I realised that her ongoing close association with the Police Force had probably been a factor in the consideration made by her nephew when he had finally agreed to pass on Julie's phone contact details to me without too much trouble.

From my side, it was pleasant to know that I had been able to impress Julie with the fact that my work had given me the opportunity to travel the world, and she was vociferously envious that my chosen career path had led to Sally and me living in South Africa for three years.

'Listen, Chilli, please call me Jules,' she said. 'Everyone does - and do tell me more about your time in South Africa. I've always wanted to go there.'

And so I did - South Africa has always held a place in my heart; some of the happiest and most memorable experiences in my life were spent in the three years I lived there.

Sally had, of course, been with me. It was before we were married, but she had risked taking a break from her job, working for the NHS in a teaching role, to come with me. Not having a work permit for South Africa, she had been the catalyst for making my work secondment such a successful and memorable experience for us both. While I was working during the normal weekdays, she was able to focus much of her time there just planning our next weekend adventure.

We spent as much time as we were able there, using whatever spare time we could find, travelling throughout Southern Africa, visiting cultural sites, game reserves, and historical points of interest, 'white water rafting in the Zambezi' and turning the whole work assignment into the most wonderful experiential, three year long holiday of a lifetime. Topping all was 'the icing on the cake' when my youngest son was born in the Sandton Hospital, in Gauteng, shortly before our eventual return to reality back in the UK.

As we meandered our conversation back into today-time, I told Julie of my search for her and how I had eventually managed to find her by simply forgetting all of the government records, etc., and just using a 'telephone book' approach, locating her through the male line of her family.

We spoke for what seemed like forever, exhausting whatever memories we could partially recall of the 'old days' and the disappointment and sadness we both shared that our friendship back then couldn't have lasted longer.

Julie said (I had difficulty, at first, in remembering her preference for being called Jules) that she had always held a theory about my family moving out of the area when they did, and as she told me, I began to see how it might have been.

Her theory was that the coming-together of her and I as close play-friends had quite understandably led to the meeting-up of both sets of our parents for one reason or another, generally to sort out problems we had created or pacify neighbours aggrieved by our escapades.

That, in turn, she surmised, had led to a relationship building between my mother and her father, or possibly it had been between both sets of parents, it didn't really matter. She felt that together they had probably been some of the earliest 'Swingers' in the area.

I can't say I was immediately taken with what she was implying, but had to accept that it certainly seemed to be one plausible explanation for how things had turned out back then. Our parents would have undoubtedly had to meet, a possible result of their two raucous off-springs, and that may have led to a close, perhaps a very close relationship. The Pampas Grass, growing in Julie's front garden, that she used in her Tonto headdress - no, surely not - 'Swingers' was something from the 1970's, wasn't it?

Maybe it was just a coincidence, or maybe they actually were 'swinging pioneers' ahead of their time.

'Tread carefully,' I told myself. I had to avoid bending facts to fit into an unsubstantiated supposition - I would need to check up on a few things before adding that into the picture Julie was building up.

My Grandmother's insistence however, that we move out of the immediate area. Moving closer to where she could keep an eye on things was a possibility, a more realistic pointer to keep in mind. The rapid decision to move to such a relatively close locality, with very little notice, and for no apparent logical reason. Certainly, there were some strong indicators that could be used to support Julie's supposition of the possible promiscuity of our respective parents.

Whatever, it was all 'water under the bridge' now. We would never know for certain, and I must admit it was not something I particularly wanted to delve too deeply into. 'Let sleeping dogs lie' and all that.

'So what now?' Julie asked. A good question.

'Well, in truth, I have enjoyed my searching experience more than I would have thought, and thinking about it, I might like to undertake a few more 'people search' challenges. Perhaps, if I feel I'm good enough, I could hire my services out to others on a 'Fee for Results' basis. Nothing too serious, just a bit of fun.'

'I heard somewhere,' Julie cut in, 'that something like over 170,000 people go missing in the UK each year. There was the Missing Persons Unit of the West Midlands Police, but their focus understandably tended to concentrate more towards circumstances where a crime or a risk of harm is involved.' She took a deep sighing breath then - 'There is the 'Salvation Army' and local charities like 'Missing People' where teams of volunteers specialise in trying to support relatives by searching for missing people throughout the UK. But again, these tend to focus their attention towards situations where people have gone missing, rather than the simpler sort of enquiry agency you are talking of, one where it is more focused towards locating past friends and acquaintances.'

Jules had obviously done a little digging of her own and sounded as if she was harbouring a few thoughts along similar lines to my own.

'I searched Wikipedia as one of my routes,' I said, 'when I was trying to locate you, and found that 'Friends Reunited,' which had focused - through a 'portfolio of social networking' - on creating reunions of past acquaintances, but that finally closed shop in February 2016. Since then, the mish-mash of alternative search channels don't appear to provide the sort of be-spoke research that I feel is sometimes needed.'

We both sat quietly for a few seconds, each waiting for the other one to carry the possibilities further forwards. I broke the silence.

'That leaves a gap for 'Enquiry Agencies' to fill and specialise in this type of research. The one or two professional Enquiry Agencies - the ones that I had looked at, as pointers for ideas as to the approach to use when looking to see how to go about locating you, all had an understandable framework of operational rules. Some of the rules were there to protect the interests of the client searching for a relative or acquaintance, and some were there to safeguard the interests of the person being searched for.'

Jules nodded her understanding, with her background in the police force; she probably knows all of this better than me, I thought.

'One factor that stands out for me, however, is the stated preference of most of these Enquiry Agents for the whereabouts of the missing person to have been known within the last six years. Also, a caveat that they wouldn't undertake searches for people missing for over twenty years.' Again Jules nodded, she was obviously thinking ahead of my rationalisation.

'This, had I wished, or could have afforded, to use the services of one of these agencies, would have been quite a frustration given that I had been looking for you, someone I had lost over seventy years earlier.'

'Perhaps,' I suggested, 'there could be a gap in the market for someone willing to work outside of any 'time limiting' restraints. If I did decide to continue along the 'people tracing' business, that might be the niche I could look to venture into.'

'Chilli Pepper's Lost and Found Friendly Enquiry Agency? I half-jokingly announced, smiling to indicate that

I might still possibly be trying to be humorous. In truth, I was looking for a 'get-out' if Jules thought my idea sounded silly.

Julie (Jules) Saltmarsh smiled. 'I think you might need to give the whole thing a bit more thought. If I might be so bold as to suggest, why not, with our combined skills and my connections and contacts throughout the Police and News Agencies, make it the 'Salt and Pepper Lost and Found Friendly Enquiry Agency?'

So, Jules wanted to join me in turning my crazy idea into reality, and, as she pointed out, having a partner with her skills and connections added to 'what little' I brought to the party held, within it, some sound logic that actually made sense.

I sat stunned for what seemed to be a long ten seconds or so, playing and replaying what Jules had said through my mind.

She smiled as she watched my lips move as I mouthed the initials through my mind.

'Salt and Pepper Lost and Found Friendly Enquiry Agency - Sap-laf-fea,' I pronounced slowly. Testing the syllables aloud.

'Sounds like an Eastern European country,' she giggled, 'We might need to do a bit of jiggery pokery on that name. Work on that a bit, but it will do for a start.' The dam of control that we had both stoically tried to keep in place broke, and rising to our feet, we hugged, clinging to each other across the table and laughing like a couple of giggling school kids.

Chapter 10 – Sap-laf-fea

28/11/22 pm

It didn't feel right to be saying goodbye so soon after all of that effort expended in trying to find Julie, and then the pent-up excitement and foreboding leading to our actual meeting. I didn't think it was just me who felt this, I sensed it was a shared feeling as we both seemed reluctant to break off from our 'coffee meet-up' and go our separate ways once again.

'Look, why don't we get together again soon? I would love for you to meet up with Sally – I think you two would hit it off, and – no joking - If you are serious, we can explore our thoughts further, if you're still up for setting up an Enquiry Agency, I mean – What was it we ended up calling it - Sap-laf-fea?' I smiled half-jokingly, 'We could dig a little deeper and see if there might be some substance for doing something along those lines. Worth taking a look, I mean, even if it goes nowhere.'

'Sounds good to me,' she said, standing up and reaching across for her coat. 'Beats the shit out of retirement, and it will be something to add to the excitement of my Pilates classes. Let's do that and not leave it another seventy years before doing so.'

I sensed that she was joking about her Pilates classes 'being exciting', but hey, I've never done it, so what do I know?

'Julie, even if Sap-laf-fea goes no further, I want to hold onto our friendship this time. I would be sad for it to waste away like I felt it did the first time.'

'Me too, you old softie,' she said, and she leaned across and gave me a peck kiss on the cheek.

'Let's meet up again early next week if you're free. It would be great if you could drive over to my place next time Jules. I would like for you to meet Sal if she is around, she has put up with a lot of my nonsense over the past couple of months while I have been searching for you.'

'I would love to,' she said, 'She must be quite something to have finally got you tamed.'

'Great, how about next Monday? In the meantime, we can both look further into what it would take to start up our very own Enquiry Agency'.

'Fine, Monday works for me.'

So that was agreed, I gave her my home address and she entered it onto her iPhone, before tucking it away in her shoulder bag.

'Monday it is then, say around 10?'

We both had plenty to 'think on' in the time before then. Neither of us had any direct contacts within the 'Private Investigator' field of business, but Jules had come across some people in that line of work during her time with the police service – however, that was some time ago - and with the NCA, but she had never really made any serious contacts, so I guess it would mean us both starting from scratch.

We both put our outdoor coats, gloves, and such on and hugged again, maybe a little more tightly and a little longer than was necessary, my beanie hat knocking her beret askew and both feeling a bit daft and a little embarrassed with all of the stares we were getting from the young mothers in the cafe. I think two old fogies hugging one another in the middle of the day, in the centre of a crowded cafe, was a mite unusual - but that was a consequence of us going seventy years without a hug. We said our goodbyes – I asked Julie if she needed a lift but was told she only lived a short walking distance from the town centre and could do with a bit of food shopping on her way home.

"And anyway, I need the exercise.'

'Go in peace, Tonto.'

'Arrivederci Kemosabe.'

And we went our separate ways, me back to my car and Julie off to do a bit of shopping on her way home. It was just starting to rain again, a quite heavy outburst. I smiled to myself, thinking, 'You silly bugger' - Jules, not me - but inwardly hoped she didn't have too far to walk in the downpour.

My drive home in the rain became quite a reflective time, thinking of all the things I should have said and all the things I should have saved to say for some other time. But 'all in all' I felt the reunion had gone well, better than I could have expected and that the original goal I had set myself, those few weeks back, of finding my earliest remembered friend had been a success. Tick that box. That Julie appeared keen to explore with me the idea of turning our meet-up into a new venture was a pleasant development and a bonus. I could never have imagined that would be the outcome when I left home that morning.

I went on to think about how I was going to explain Sap-laf-fea to Sally. I had – half-jokingly – mentioned to Sal the concept as a bit of a joke in the early days when I had first started this search, but now it was beginning to look like it might actually be a possibility. How would she take it? She would probably tell me not to be such an old fool.

When I arrived home, I saw that Sal had left me a note to say she was out having her hair styled, wouldn't be back until around five pm and could I start making something for tea?

After my meeting with Julie, I was still bubbling and couldn't really get too worked up about having to cook an evening meal. What I really fancied was fish, chips and mushy pees tonight. I was pretty sure that it wouldn't take too much to convince Sally, when she got back, that we should celebrate my meeting with Julie, by having a take-away from the local fish and chips shop.

Also, my walk there, with Truffle, would tick her 'evening walkies' box. I could then, when I got back, fill Sally in on the details of the meeting, while we ate.

And that's what happened.

Surprisingly she took the news better than I had thought would happen. I had, in truth, expecting a negative reaction, being told I was too old and being daft for thinking of pursuing the thought of becoming a private 'enquiry agent', but to my surprise, her reaction was, 'As long as you keep your household jobs in order, fine. It will keep you out of my hair.'

'Nice hair', I said, 'Is that from the new hairdressers by the Post Office?'

'You're fooling no one with the false flattery Chilli Pepper – just don't let this new thing take over all of your time and make sure Truffle gets her walkies.'

Chapter 11 - Ground Rules and Games

Monday 5th December

Julie and I met up again the following Monday as agreed. She had driven over to our village in her tiny little yellow Smart car. As planned, it was a day when Sally was working from home, which allowed her to join us for a brief spell and finally meet my childhood friend, the woman who had been the centre point of my attention for the past month or so.

There was quite a chill in the air that morning, I had planned for us all to go over to the small café, a short walk away from our house, but the log fire, which I had lit for the first time this winter was too much of a draw to move away from.

I wasn't sure how this meeting would go, but once the two ladies had shaken hands and passed a few of the usual introductory pleasantries, they both seemed to settle into a comfortable chat together on the sofa in front of the wood burner.

It was probably in the nature of the two ladies that they both recognised something in one another that let them easily relax and feel comfortable together. They seemed more like old friends than new acquaintances, and the next quarter of an hour was spent with the usual incidental and nonsensical chit-chat about the weather, our kids etc., before finally turning into a diatribe between the two new friends about 'what a pain I had been at home' in my search for Jules.

I sat there, hardly saying a word unless asked to by one or the other. I learned that they both apparently liked Michael Bublé, going on train journeys, cats and travelling abroad - What more to life was there?

Eventually, Sal turned the conversation back to my recent obsession with locating Julie.

'He has been like a bear with a sore head, ask him to do anything around the house and be prepared for some sarky comment to make it sound like I was bullying him. Manipulating bugger.'

I didn't remember that.

'No change there, then. He was just like that back in those days - a sulky child searching for his lost teddy', Jules threw in.

'Would you two ladies like a cup of tea and some chocolate digestives?' I asked.

'That would be lovely.' They both said at the same time. Then carried on with their inane derogatory chattering.

I made the tea and put a packet of biscuits on the tray. They talked.

It was as if I had become a surplus appendage to the 'coming together' of two old school friends. 'Best to let them get comfortable with one another', I thought, so just smiled, nodded whenever they looked my way, nursed my tea, and let them witter away about anything and everything.

Finally, after a quarter of a cup of tea, Sal brought matters back to what we had really met up to talk over.

'How serious are you two about properly doing this 'people search' business as more than just a hobby?' She asked.

Julie and I glanced at each other, then both started to speak at the same time.

'Well, I'm up for giving it a go' mixed with 'Yes, why not?' as we both spoke, the excitement in our voices showing through.

'Okay then, might I suggest you need to get some shape into things? What you can do and what you can't. Chilli, you know all about that sort of process planning stuff. You did it for long enough.'

She was right, of course. What was needed was some structure, a framework we could all agree to work within. Sal wouldn't be able to be fully involved, but all recognised that whatever we did would undoubtedly have an impact upon her. So there needed to be an agreed shape to things.

Something we could fall back on if actions looked like they were moving out of our control or intended purpose.

I explained that 'Not knowing - really knowing that is - where to start when setting up an Enquiry Agency and without the benefit of any advice from anyone already 'in the business', I have started to read whatever I can find online. To that, I have tried to apply whatever I felt fitted in from my past business experience to try to get some logic into our proposed undertaking. My aim is to make sure Julie and I, if we are to do this, are fully aligned in our thinking and intentions, why we are doing it and what our desired outcome is.'

Julie was happy with that – 'Things have to take second place to the work I still do for the NCA, of course - but that still leaves me with plenty of time on my hands. I can start touching base with a few of my contacts still working within the police and the legal professions just to make sure that whatever we decide keeps within what was required by law.' She stopped talking for a second or two, looking as if she were giving it a bit of thought.

'I'm pretty sure that the fact that we intend to do this 'people searching business' as a charitable undertaking, will - in general - lead to the authorities being supportive. But there again, that is a further reason for there needing to be a clear set of rules guiding all involved in what we can and can't do.'

'I think I will set the concept of the 'start-up' of a new charity as a short one-week project for the students in my Business Studies class at the college.' Sal thew in. 'It will be a useful piece of learning and research work for them, and it might unearth something you haven't thought of.'

That was good to hear - the fact that Sal was actively joining in with what we were proposing - even if her idea didn't provide any meaningful outcomes - which I didn't think it would - showed she was comfortable with and supportive of what we were proposing.

We chatted about all sorts of things for the next hour or so, and then Jules said that she had a few things to tidy up back home. So each with our own little tasks to do, Sal and I said our goodbyes to Jules, and off she tootled in her little yellow Smart Car. I couldn't hold back a smile as I watched her drive away, as she brought back to mind that vintage children's programme that used to be on the BBC, where Noddy and Big Ears would always end their adventures by driving away in their little yellow car.

So it was all actually going to happen, I think in the heart of me, I hadn't really thought it would, but it was, and we Three Musketeers were ready to begin the next phase of our new challenge.

Once we were alone again, I asked Sally for her true thoughts and opinion of what we were planning.

'I'm on board with it, I really am. I think Jules is great - very thorough and logical in her approach to things. She won't let you make a complete ass of yourself. But 'my God' what a turn up of the books though.'

'What do you mean?' I asked.

'She is the spitting image of you. Make your legs a foot shorter, lose five stone in weight, shave off your beard, grow your hair down to your shoulders and put you in a dress, and you two could pass for twin sisters!' she giggled. 'She's like your 'Mini-Me'; she's lovely.'

'Wouldn't that mean I'd need to grow my bust and learn to like Michael Bublé first, though?' I countered. But there it was again, that fleeting concern - albeit not something I gave voice to - that there might be just a glimmer of possibility in Sal's comments about Jules and I - thoughts of pampas grass and wayward parents, briefly flashing through my mind. After all, accepting the possibility of Julie's supposition that the relationship between her parents and mine could have been closer than I might like to imagine. Then extending that supposition back in time to when both couples might first have become friends, it was plausible that some familial transgressions may have taken place and, if so, Jules and I might possibly be related.

'Rubbish' - it didn't bear thinking about, and I wasn't going to take the matter any further. I didn't want to know if I was right or wrong with that crazy line of thinking; Jules and I were not brother and sister, we were just good friends, and that was the way it was and the way I wanted to leave it.

I determined to give it no more thought. I went through the habitual routine of stroking and feeding both cats rubbing my faithful dog's tummy and finally getting around to taking off my coat. Then settling into the sofa in the front room, opened up my laptop and set to work.

Sal had a dental appointment, so not long after Jules left, so she nipped upstairs to brush her teeth, before wrapping up warmly and setting off to the dentist's.

Straight into it, while fresh on my mind, I started noting my ideas down in writing. After quite a few rethinks and rewrites, and with a little help from Sally on her return from the dental check-up - I drafted out an initial set of rules and principles for our new venture.

I went through with Sally what I had set out in my initial draft - she was a good sounding board, small things I might have missed or may not have considered relevant she picked up on, and pretty soon, we had something I felt good enough as a draft for discussion, the next time we all met up.

I emailed a copy of the suggested rules and principles to Jules later that same day. We weren't due to meet up again for another week, but I thought it would give her some time to look through what I had suggested and maybe come up with a few thoughts of her own.

I altered, added to, refined, and tweaked the rules throughout the following week.

'You're like a cat worrying a mouse', Sal told me more than once. 'Put it down and forget about it until you speak with Jules next.'

She was right, of course, but there wasn't anything around to take my mind off it, so I kept going back, adding bits, or taking them out.

Our next 'coffee shop' meet-up was again on a Monday, a week or so later. It was there that I finally got to go over my suggestions with Jules making it clear that this was just an initial stab at it and - no doubt - things would evolve and adapt further over time once we were 'up and running' and more aware of what likely issues we might incur.

There were only a few changes that had remained from my constant tweaks over that past week, and most changes had gone in one day, only to have been taken out the next.

Sally was tied up in a team meeting at the college all day and had left home that morning pretty racked off, annoyed and complaining about what she felt would have been a far more productive use of her and all of her colleague's time had their meeting taken place 'online'.

So, it was just Julie and I at a different coffee shop in Kenilworth this time. We found a table tucked away in the corner of the cafe, and I went through each of the points, rules, suggestions, whatever, explaining what was meant in each instance and why I felt the need to have it written out and agreed.

I explained that I felt it would be necessary to review these rules periodically, specifically after the first couple of investigations. We needed to ensure that they continued to reflect what we personally wanted to get out of this business enterprise. And we had to continue to ensure that what we were doing was providing a beneficial service for those clients that needed our help.

Jules accepted most of what I was suggesting and asked a few questions to make sure she fully understood the point I was making, and why I felt it to be relevant, and with just a few small adjustments, we agreed it would be a good 'start point', something that we could both work with, during our start-up phase.

So we agreed;

1. We will not accept any requests for investigations or enquiries that risk placing us in a conflicting position with either the Police or the National Crime Agency. If any active investigations look to be moving towards that particular area of responsibility, we will review our

position and, if relevant, pass our findings on to the appropriate authority. (I had to respect Jules' ongoing role within the NCA and recognise the fact that we were, certainly at this early point in our undertakings, just a well-meaning group of 'do-gooders' and, with the exception of Sally, all on the wrong side of seventy).

2. Work must be worthwhile and enjoyable in the broadest sense. Our clients need to benefit from our undertakings, and we will aim to end each day with a smile. (Sounds a bit soft, but it would be something we both felt we might need to remind each other about as things progressed).

3. Not for profit, initially. (Jules insisted I add the word 'initially', and it made sense) But we must aim, wherever possible, to recover, or at least minimise our expenses.

4. Keep it local, e.g., Coventry, Kenilworth, Leamington, Warwick, Stratford and surrounding villages. (This was tied to the previous point, it being impractical for us to try to operate outside of the local area).

5. Avoid any and all physical altercations, but 'be prepared. We are too old for any of that crap. (I wasn't just thinking of self-defence here, I also felt that it was important we both had a basic awareness of first aid and resuscitation training. At our age, we needed to be practical in our awareness and mindful of our health limitations).

6. Important decisions that affect our activities, or individuals in the team, can only be taken where there are 'no objections' from any of the team. Trust will only emerge if consensus is based on a thorough understanding of each other's interests and concerns.

7. We will focus and concentrate our resources on just one client at a time until we feel able to cope with a rethink.

8. Our prime focus is to work on locating missing people and/or lost objects.

9. All prior commitments to other parties must come first. (This took into consideration any family matters, Julie's ongoing relationship with the NCA and Sally's work with the college. It was important that I accept that there were certain things that Julie would be prohibited from doing because of her ongoing involvement with the NCA.)

10. We are a team and must always strive to make the most appropriate use of the skills and abilities of the team. (No room for heroes).

'I think that should do for a start.' I said, 'Ten rules are enough. I don't think we should tie ourselves up with too many restrictions from the outset. We are a small team, and we just need to act sensibly, and respect each other's needs, responsibilities, and prior commitments, if we are to gel. We can always go back and add or amend these rules after we have worked with the ten for a while.' I told her.

'Thinking about what you said,' Julie put in, 'with regard to the last rule - the one about striving to make the best use of our abilities - I don't think we should start advertising or publicly promoting our venture too loudly yet. Let's start slow. Let it be known locally that we are just a small team of people with certain 'search and find' skills and abilities and that we are prepared to use these abilities to help people in need of our services.'

'Ha ha', I thought, 'You're as nervous as me about this little venture! Good, that is as it should be - 'slowly-slowly' to get things started, not biting off more than we can chew.'

I didn't say anything but nodded my agreement.

On reflection and looking back on it now, I note that by the sixth rule, I was already talking in terms of teams! Getting ahead of myself again! At that moment, it was just Jules and me, with, of course, a little support, guidance and encouragement from Sally. But both Jules and I agreed that, for all important decisions, Sal must be included within our 'Team' classification.

'Listen, I've got a friend, someone I've worked with in the National Crime Agency for a good few years now. I've told him about what it is we were thinking about doing, and he's said he very much liked our idea about setting up a 'Not for Profit' Enquiry Agency. His name is Mal, and he is - believe me - an 'out and out' wiz with computers, the internet, search engines and all that gubbins.' All of this was rattled out at 90 miles an hour, she hardly seemed to take a breath. 'And he's retired, like us. I'm pretty sure he is bored to tears with sitting at home watching his goldfish. He's still on active call from the NCA as a Special, but they seldom use him now. They've got kids now, who look no older than thirteen, working for them on their computer stuff.'

'Just take a breath Jules and slow down,' I thought, but kept it to myself.

Her friend apparently was a guy by the name of Malcom Strange. He had retired from the police force around the same time as Jules, and from what Jules was saying, it sounded like he was more than just a little bit interested in the service we were looking to provide. A possible early recruit to join our, currently non-existing, agency? Maybe. With someone like that in the team, it would certainly close a gap in our internet search capabilities!

At that time, I hadn't realised what a diamond this guy would turn out to be, but I'm jumping ahead of myself here.

In my mind, I went back to Rule 5, the one dealing with safety and self-defence. It was, I felt, something that needed to be looked at seriously. Jules had undertaken rudimentary self-defence, first aid and resuscitation training while working within the police services, but that was some time back and apart from a few early 'after hours' scuffles in the days when she was 'walking the beat', forty-something years ago, she had never experienced any situations that had called on her to use either of those skills in earnest.

As for myself, I could definitely benefit from some formal first-aid training. I was okay when it came to putting a plaster on a cut, and blood didn't upset me, but that about summed it up. As far as self-defence was concerned, I did have some history I could fall back on there. I had a fair bit of experience in martial arts training right up to and into my later years.

Having played school and then club rugby from the age of eleven, right through to my mid-forties, I was used to a few occasional physical altercations. However, apart from one brief 'drink-related' scuffle with one of our second team props at the rugby club disco night, towards the end of my playing days, it was on the rugby pitch that I had probably thrown my last punch in earnest. Club rugby, in the Midlands and probably all over the UK back in those days, was quite often the setting for a few 'manly fist flare ups'. It came with the game, never amounted to more than the odd bloody nose, and tended to end up in the bar after the game when you bought your adversary a pint.

Thinking back now, I will recall that one scuffle I did get into, at the Corby Rugby Club disco all those years back, I could never have imagined the part it would play in my life so many years later, but it helps set the scene for what was to happen later.

The incident was nothing really to write home about. One of our second team props, quite a big, heavy-set bloke, was something of a bully, both on and off the pitch. Always playing 'Mr Hard Man' and looking for someone smaller, or more popular in the club, to ridicule or intimidate. I had tried to avoid his company as far as possible, and that might have been part of the cause for the growing dislike he had for me.

The night when our little altercation happened was back in the late 70's. I clearly remember that the record we were dancing to was Queen's 'Fat Bottom Girls' and the dancefloor was crowded with quite boisterous rugby players and their partners. Everyone was laughing and prancing about like idiots, whilst shouting along, at the top of our voices, with the lyrics to the song. Then, out of the blue, for no earthly reason I could think of, this prop Tim Goodfellow, gave me a good shove in the back, making me stumble forward into the girl I was dancing with. I turned, still smiling and thinking it was an accident, but Goodfellow just stood there grinning maliciously at me, his fists clenched.

'Outside you bastard, I'm gonna knock your fuckin head off.'

That came out of the blue, I had no idea what had brought this on, but I guess that too much beer mixed with the long-held grudge he had against me for some obscure reason, had finally pushed him to the point where he was going to take me down a peg or two.

I'd had a few beers myself, and enough was enough, time to put a stop to the ongoing friction that had festered for too long between us. I'd tried being friendly with the twat in the past, but that wasn't working, and in truth, I had, in the back of my mind, sensed that the time would come sooner rather than later when we would have to settle matters between us. Lance the boil, so to say. That time was now!

The dancing all around stopped, everyone was looking at Goodfellow and me.

'Come on then, outside,' I said, turning and starting to walk towards the door.

As I turned my back on him, he swung his fist at me, but fortunately another of our team, a tall second-row Geordie, had been dancing with his wife nearby and he reached out, catching Goodfellow's arm and deflecting his punch sufficiently so as to only lightly glance off my shoulder.

My knee-jerk reaction was impulsive, the fight was not going to be outside in the carpark, it was happening now.

Without time to think, I retaliated with a punch of my own, connecting with the side of Goodfellow's head and knocking him sideways. He kept to his feet, but I could see that my retaliation had not been expected. Not only was it a shock, but it had also rocked the centre point of his balance, he was dizzy, and his eyes were looking more than a little unfocused.

It ended there, my Geordie buddy and a couple of the other guys in the room stepped in between us and the incident, apart from some not unexpected and highly crude expletives on Goodfellow's part, seemed to have blown over. But I knew only too well that this would be a grudge Goodfellow would never forget. I had got the last punch in, and he had 'lost face' and was definitely coming off worse from the incident.

Still, having stood my ground with him, going forwards, I was no longer on his 'to be bullied list', and from then on he kept his distance away from me and focused on some other poor souls who he felt he could more easily intimidate physically either on or off the pitch and that, I had hoped, was the end of the matter.

This was about the time of my last full season of playing club rugby. I was into my forties, no longer in the first team and having to accept that, whilst I still loved the game, I was too old for all those Saturday afternoon knocks and exertions.

It was a big wrench; I had been playing the game for well over twenty years. An overseas work assignment, the one that took Sally and me to South Africa for a while, and other commitments took precedence over that side of my life.

It wasn't until a number of years later that I started looking again for some form of organised sporting activity. It was Sally who had been badgering me to look for some type of physical activity I could, not only watch, but participate in, with our son Marcus.

Marcus had just turned seven and was too young for mini rugby, but old enough to learn one of the martial arts.

Tang Soo Do was our chosen path, a Korean discipline based on Karate. Why Tang Soo Do? Well, the simple answer was that it was the only Karate training classes I could find close to where we lived.

So, twice a week, it became father and son time at the gym, without mothers or sisters to bother. Father and son, bonding time.

Together we spent the next four and a half years or so, one night and one Saturday afternoon a week, earning our black belts in karate.

Marcus had taken to it like a duck to water, learning the rules and various Hyung (forms) quicker than I ever could (a younger mind, I guess) and earning his second Dan by the time he turned twelve.

Twelve was a decisive age to reach for Marcus. It was when he realised school rugby, theatre club, and girls held a greater attraction than karate classes with dad. Probably my constant frustration and moaning about how complicated and pointless some of the set forms were, didn't help either.

I soldiered on, on my own, with karate for a short time, but in truth, I didn't enjoy it as much without Marcus, and the constant focus on having to perfect predetermined Hyung forms finally got to me. So, not wanting to give up a disciplined training programme altogether, I switched my allegiance over to what my ex-karate buddies would have called the 'dark side' and joined a Krav Maga group. Now well into my sixties, I stuck with Krav for five or six years until along came COVID, effectively putting a stop for a time on all contact sports.

I never went back to Krav Maga. It was a milestone, I had turned seventy and had moved on, I guess, mellowing a little, growing-up and finally recognising I was too old for this sort of thing.

So what did this all mean? Well I guess it is fair to say overall that I have a fair experience in martial arts. But that needs to be balanced with the fact that I am 'no spring chicken' and while it might sound like the right sort of background needed for an Enquiry Agent, in all honesty, all it had tended to do, in the past, was make me a shade over-confident in those odd 'tricky situations' where I probably would have been better advised to take a more cautious approach. Sal and my two youngest kids have, on more than a few occasions over the years, tried - usually successfully - to get me to 'take a step back' and 'not get involved' in some minor awkward situation or other that could and should easily have been avoided.

Again it was time for me to accept reality, being in my seventies, I was just a wee bit too old for putting myself in situations beyond which my body, or heart, would support.

Now, should Jules and I face the possibility of innocently walking into an unwelcome situation, it was more important we accept the limitations that age had put upon us.

'Better to plan things through beforehand, rather than in hindsight!' was best self-defence approach needed. But it was something I knew I would struggle with.

The 'be prepared' bit - well, apart from the first aid side of things - Jules told me she always carried a personal alarm attached to her tote bag shoulder strap and a pocket size can of a legal alternative to pepper spray in the bag itself. And for me, all I currently had was a broken wooden stool leg in the boot of my car, a remnant from South Africa.

When Sal and I had finally taken the decision to return to the UK, my work buddies in the Midrand office on the outskirts of Johannesburg had bought us two fold-away tripod stools, made from leather and wood, as a leaving present. I'm not sure what animal the leather came from, but the wooden tripod legs, I was told, were made from leadwood, a type of wood so heavy and dense that it sinks in water. Whether or not this was true, the fashioned wooden legs were certainly disproportionately heavy for what one would have normally thought they should weigh.

Moving into our new house in the village back in the UK, the two stools became a part of our garden room furniture. Somehow, I don't recall how or when, I managed to break one of the tripod legs on one of the stools. It had snapped at the point where the pivot screws were drilled through to join all three legs together.

The broken stool sat for a couple of years, tucked away in the garden shed, until I finally got around to fixing it, just a few months back. I was quite pleased with the job I had made of the repair, using a piece of wood cut from an old broom pole of a similar diameter. The broken leadwood stool leg, which was about the length of my forearm, looked and felt like it would make a weighty truncheon should it ever be needed. And, feeling quite attached to it, just a bit of meaningless sentimentality, I left it in the boot of my car, telling myself that I might need it one day.

As a defensive weapon, or thug deterrent, it would be pretty useless, I guess. I couldn't - in all practicality – openly carry it around with me, and residing in the boot of my car - I thought at that time - would make it almost impossible to get to should the time ever come when I would need it most. It was simply a 'big boy's toy', but still I felt irrationally attached to it, so a good enough reason for keeping it.

Recognising that it would make more sense to follow Jules' example and invest in some sort of alarm device and spray can, I decided to order some things online.

I had in the back of my mind that Mace, or other similar pepper sprays, are illegal in the UK, so I would need to find an alternative product such as the one Jules carried. Hers was a red dye spray specifically designed as a deterrent. Small enough to fit in a coat pocket, and available to purchase 'online' through Amazon. The dye was designed to temporarily stain the assailant's skin without causing any longer-term physical harm.

Probably good enough, I accepted; while it wouldn't immobilise a would-be attacker, being sprayed with red dye would be an effective deterrent to all but the most aggressive thug, making them think again and - if I were near to my car and could get to it - my broken stool leg would do the rest!

Putting that to one side, Jules suggested we worked on building up our skills and abilities. Starting small we began by doing some self-training - people searches. Setting challenges for one another - using whatever means available, through church records, telephone directories, 'search engines', or whatever we needed to employ, without - at this stage - spending any money in locating friends and relations who weren't really missing. Practice, simulation runs so to say, making a game of it and having some fun.

We agreed to meet up and start our practice searches in earnest each Wednesday, which in the beginning, for the first week or so, we managed to keep to. But the game was soon becoming obsessive, and what started out as a once-a-week 'self-training exercise' proved to be too much fun to leave off dabbling with. Also, after the second weekly meeting, we accepted that, while one 'formal get together' just once a week might be useful for swapping ideas and learning, we were both finding ourselves throughout the week, whenever we could sneak away from household tasks, distracted and stealing time away to work on our fun training assignments.

Christmas had come and gone since our first meeting following the coffee shop reunion, and we were now actively training to be PI's (Private Investigators) in earnest. Albeit I still preferred the term Enquiry Agents as I believed it set us apart from those professional PI's whose work required them to stay up all night or sneak around taking photos of misbehaving marriage partners.

I didn't intend to belittle true PI's (notice I didn't then count our small team as being in that role yet), I just felt we were too old for creeping around dark alleys at night and that sort of business. I was pretty keen we step back from that side of things and focus our attention solely on tracing those missing people who wouldn't object to being found, if possible. At least that, I felt, was challenging and rewarding enough to start with - nothing too strenuous, and it meant we could manage our workdays and I would get to sleep in my own bed, with Sal, at night.

Chapter 12 – Malware

Julie's friend Malcom Strange - 'Call me Mal', as he told us - had joined the team about three weeks into our 'people search' game and just a week or so before Christmas.

Before our actual meeting, I have to admit that from the short conversations Jules and I had previously, with regard to Mal, I'd formed a mental picture of someone with a fixation on computer technology, who would be difficult for me to relate to.

I soon found out I was wrong. Mal was quite a personable guy, someone I found easy to get on with and truly 'worth his weight in gold' when it came to computer-aided searches. Like Jules and I, he was in his early seventies. A shortish guy, I'd say around five foot seven or eight tall (I still struggle with metric measurement), slim and wiry, mostly grey-haired now of course, almost white, but with just a trace of what once must have been ginger showing in his moustache and neatly trimmed little goatee beard.

He lived in the old mining village of Keresley, now a district on the outskirts of Coventry. The colliery had been closed as a part of Maggie Thatcher's green eco-strategy back in the early 1990's, but the workforce and their families, those who had put down roots in the area, remained.

Attracted to the area just after the end of the First World War, had a large contingent of Welsh and Scottish miners had come to work the pit. And there was something about the way Mal spoke, the phrases he used, the ways in which he expressed himself, the rounding of his words, that gave me the impression that his family had originated from somewhere north of Hadrian's Wall.

He told me that his grandfather, his father, and his uncles had all worked in the colliery, and he had felt that there had been something like a sense of disappointment within the family circle when, after leaving school and working for a brief spell in the colliery offices, he had left to join the Police Force.

'It was almost as if I had deserted the family clan and gone over to the 'other side.'

He was a dapper guy always, Jules had told me, taking pride and care with his appearance. When we first met, he was dressed smartly in a dark maroon and blue striped tie, neatly pressed chinos, with a contrastingly designed plaid waistcoat, and well-polished black leather Oxford shoes. As it was our first meeting, I had assumed he had purposefully dressed up for the occasion, but Jules assured me, once we were alone, that Mal had always been the same ever since she had first known him over twenty years back.

I sensed Mal, who was apparently divorced and single, held something of a flame for Jules. He always addressed her as Julie, or Mrs Saltmarsh – never Jules when talking about her with Sal and me - and I noted, he almost seemed to stand, or sit to attention, when she came into a room. She had been paired up with Mal, by the NCA, on a number of investigations when they were both required to work some complex cases, Jules had told me. It seemed that this close working relationship had developed and grown into a strong, trusting bond between them.

'He specialises in cybercrime and has an MBA and a Degree in Computer Science.' I was informed. 'He's a genius at Computer Forensics and Cyber Security. Does a lot of that sort of work for the NCSC.'

She must have seen the glaze coming over my eyes because she added, 'The National Cyber Security Centre, they still call on him when they get a difficult problem on their hands. He has a great sense of humour for a computer geek. Tells everyone his specialism is in Penetration Testing.'

I guessed that passes for humour in the Geek Brigade.

'The crew in the old NCA team call him Malware,' again something connected to his work, I guess, 'never really dug into it. I know he does a bit of work for a few local businesses; I've heard he is not short of a bob or two, lucrative side-line to be in, I assume.'

'Good on him,' I thought – still, I did find it easy to like the guy. He had played club rugby in his younger days, so there was an immediate bond. That he was prepared to take on this work, with us, without the expectation of it earning him a living was another plus point.

From his lack of height and the general shape of him, I guessed he must have played in the three-quarters, probably a fly-half. It turned out I was right. He told me he had played for the local village side throughout the seventies, and, low and behold, fly-half was his position. 'Nice shot, Sherlock' - (or words to that effect) - the inner detective in me beginning to show through? Well, maybe just a shade too soon to claim that for certain!

Mal was polite to the extreme, never swore, was always prepared to say his piece and, from all accounts, had received a fair amount of self-defence training in his time as a policeman. More importantly, from my standpoint and the little I knew of computers, search engines, and the like, I accepted that he was an expert who certainly knew his business.

He had a married daughter, who now lived in the Earlsdon district of Coventry, and he proudly informed us that he was the grandfather of two boys, both of whom played rugby for the local team. He also had a granddaughter, Jess.

'Jess is,' he told us, 'better with computers than I am.'

'She is actually quite high on the Autism spectrum (ASD) and needs specialist support, through a care home in Birmingham, throughout the week to help her cope. But if I ever get a problem with a computer programme, I go to her, and nine times out of ten, she's a wiz, she can set me in the right direction.'

'Useful to know,' I thought. 'Something to store away, maybe a little gem to turn to, if future needs dictate.'

'She stays in the care home or at home with her parents most of the time, but usually comes to stay with me for a couple of days, for one weekend, each month. This helps her parents out a little and lets me enjoy some time interacting with her. That usually means us both sitting in front of our computers, I'm afraid!

It might sound a bit strange to other people, but I really enjoy those times, I guess I must also feature somewhere on the autistic spectrum myself. We just shack up with our computers playing whatever computer games are currently in vogue.'

Mal was happy with the 'Ground Rules' we had come up with so far. Didn't think we needed to make any changes at this point in time and thought what we were doing in our practice search games were a good start in helping us identify where the 'bugs were'.

'I'm keen to make a start, it all sounds like it could be a lot of fun and a chance for me to put my learning to some practical use rather than wasting my time away just gaming.'

All good to hear.

Again that uncomfortable feeling started to worry me. I was beginning to feel, a little nervously, that this was all going a bit too smoothly. Wondering if maybe we were racing ahead of ourselves a little too quickly here (always the worrier, looking for holes in the plan). Maybe we needed to think things through a little more before we kicked things off? I decided not to share my concerns with the rest of the team, not just yet – they were 'on a high' and needed me 'bringing them back down to Earth' like I needed a hole in the head.

Sal snapped me out of my worries and away from any seeds of doubt and concern I had presently.

'He is just what you need,' she informed me, 'Apart from being at home with computers, he gives you someone you can connect with and talk to on something other than work, on a social basis.'

'Rugger, you mean?'

'Yup,' she said. A slight hesitation then. 'You might also learn a little bit about what to wear and how to dress with a little bit more care. He, unlike someone I might mention, spends a little more time caring about how he looks, what he wears and when he gets up in the morning.'

I was nonplussed, I couldn't think what to say, so I thought it best to pretend I hadn't heard that last remark.

Jules was as pleased as punch that Mal had opted to join the team.

'I told you so, I knew you'd like him. He's a bloody star with computers (I had recognised that already), and he's not like you – he's polite, a gentleman, and a real pleasure to be with!'

'Where did that last bit come from?' I wondered to myself.

Sal didn't defend me, she just sat there smiling, and I was beginning to sense something of a conspiracy taking place here. Just a bit of fun I'm sure; I could live with it.

By the end of that first month of playing our search game, on which each of us was now spending about twenty hours a week, Jules, Mal and I were getting pretty good at finding each other's friends and other nominated people we had tasked each other to find. We rated each search from Easy to Extremely Hard on a zero to ten scale weighting based on various factors, which included - 'Last known whereabouts - family name and chosen profession. Of the twenty-one people we had together looked for, on an individual basis, we had between us found fifteen, all within the set 'five-day search' window.

'Not bad,' I thought, even if some of the claimed successes weren't all quite what I felt to be strictly 'kosher'. After all, we had been treating it more as a fun competition, each trying to better the others, and I was confident if we were working together as a team, on the searches, we would without doubt, improve upon that success rate.

I also had to accept that the other two were much better than me in the search work. That was no surprise, it had been their background work for forty to fifty years, and I was relatively new to this sort of work - but I was learning fast.

Word had gotten out to some of our friends of what we were doing, we hadn't tried to keep it secret, so it had helped 'spread the word' on the chance of picking up real clients. Also, one or two of the people we knew had expressed an interest in joining in and playing the 'search game.' By putting 'real searches' - carefully selected, of course, out to the wider public, it might open up a new possibility. We could – as I say, with care – quite easily switch on a much larger search team just by expanding our 'game' to other bored pensioners. We might - well, Mal might - even be able to provide a little training and guidance to those who joined up.

My daughter Jane's boyfriend Si designed computer games, a 'Programmer' of some sort - not that I actually understood what that all meant. I thought I must, at some time, have a word with him to explore opportunities. But he, like her, was currently a student at the Royal Academy of Music (RAM), so he was living in temporary accommodation, a rented student flat in London and not easily contactable. I was racing ahead of myself again, better just to keep things simple for the time being, and, at that time, I had not truly appreciated the stroke of fortune which had already come our way through Jules' friend Mal. Still, it does no harm to have more than one expert that can be called on when needed. Things definitely were starting to take shape.

But there I go again, racing away with things, as usual!

-0-0-0-

Everything went onto 'hold' over the Christmas period. Jane came home from her studies at RAM, and Marcus came home from his flat in Bristol. With visiting girlfriends and boyfriends, it was quite a busy but fun time. It was always good having the kids home for a short while, just long enough for us to enjoy their company, before their late lie-ins, messy bedrooms, and piles of 'dirty' clothes scattered around the house began to get under my skin.

Truffle was in her element with all of the people visiting, making a fuss of her and giving her tummy rubs. It was a good Christmas, one of the best, and a welcome time for us all to relax and put the projects and challenges ahead 'on hold'.

As can be expected, there was quite a bit of frivolous discussion and a fair amount of joking around Dad's crazy idea of setting up an Enquiry Agency. However, both kids had a go at our 'Search Game,' and I believe, secretly enjoyed themselves.

Jane was adamant that, if I was serious about this, I needed to do some advertising and marketing to promote our agency. I tried explaining that I felt we needed to get a little more practical experience under our belts before taking it down a commercial route and preferred letting things evolve gradually for the time being.

'For the present, I am happy with 'word of mouth' informal advertising until we have grown in confidence and experience and built up our confidence in how best to bring our capabilities into play.'

But she was right; if I were serious about finding clients, we would, at some point in the near future, need to promote our presence and spread the word more widely about what it was we were offering.

However, little did I know that things were about to take off, and it was from my initial approach to informal advertising that our first 'real' commissioned investigation was about to take place.

Chapter 13 – The 3C's

Around once a month, at the most six weeks or so, and always on a Thursday evening, I met up with a group of the guys I used to play club rugger with for a curry. We had christened ourselves the 'Corley Curry Club' or the '3C's'.

There are around twenty or so of us veterans in the '3C's', and each time, usually around a dozen or so of the group would meet up for a curry and catch up on life's happenings. Most of the guys were now in retirement or were filling in their time with part-time jobs, but sometimes they brought their sons along, as I would occasionally do with my two oldest boys (now men, both in their late forties).

It was a male-only gathering, not for any misogynistic reasons, it was just that there had not been any females playing rugby in our team back in our 'glory days', and whilst sons were allowed, no one had ever thought to bring their wives or daughters along. As a group, we are just a bunch of old blokes who, on the odd occasion, enjoy behaving like raucous teenagers. We had all played in the same team at some time or other and knew each other well, so there was always plenty of good-natured barracking going on.

Pete Tanger, also known by his mates as 'Tango' - something associated with the ginger mop of hair he had back when he was younger, no doubt – was the organiser. He acted as the centre point in agreeing where and when we would meet. We were all welcome to offer our suggestions as to where to eat, but all also happy in letting Tango take final lead and make the booking.

With the food, the company, and a just modicum of alcohol – never more than the 'driving limit' of course - unless you were lucky enough to have arranged for your wife to drop you off and pick you up - it was always a good night out.

It was on one of these curry evenings - a Thursday night - not long into the new year, that Pete, who I happened to be sitting next to, mentioned that he had heard of what I was doing in searching out missing people and things.

He had been a detective sergeant with the West Midlands Police before retiring a few years back, and I had already registered that he would be a good source for advice, in the future, should I need to call on it.

'Listen, Chilli,' he spoke quietly so as to avoid the conversation going beyond the two of us. 'I've heard about your new project, which sounds great, I might want to help out sometime if you need some help. Not now though, too busy with things, but I think I might know someone, connected with the rugger club, who could do with your assistance.'

'Pete, why don't you give me a ring tomorrow?' I told him. 'Now's not the right time or place to go into it here; too many people about, and I need to concentrate on my curry.'

I wasn't being awkward, just trying to keep our conversation private, focus on enjoying my curry, the good-natured insults and banter, and recalling old 'battlefield stories.'

'Yep, understood. I'll give you a call in the morning.' He agreed, and I filed our chat away in the back of my mind and got on with enjoying the evening.

I must admit the next day, I only half-remembered the conversation Pete and I had the night before, something to do with someone connected with the Rugby Club possibly needing my help.

But, true to his word, Pete called me around 8 am the next morning, and the story began to unfold.

'Hi Chilli, how's the head this morning?'

'A bit bloody early, isn't it? I was expecting to sleep in a bit longer this morning. I'm okay, I didn't drink like you did last night – some of us don't have wives prepared to chauffeur us about - thanks for giving me a call.'

'Some of us don't have wives anymore.' he retorted - 'Said I would call, didn't I? Not one to make false promises me, even when I'm seven-sheets-to-the-wind.'

I had forgotten he had gone through a messy divorce some years back, but my indiscretion didn't seem to have caused him any noticeable bother.

We chatted a bit longer, recalling some of the outlandish things that had been said or done the previous evening. Then Pete brought the matter around to the reason for his early morning call to me;

'Chilli, have you got your sensible hat on? I promised I would give you a call.'

'Yes, for sure. What's the story? Something to do with a missing person you wanted my lot to help find?' I asked.

'Yes, that,' he hesitated for a moment then, 'I need a serious chat with you about that if you're up for it.'

'All ears, you have my attention.'

'Okay, you remember Sam White, the black guy who used to come up the club with his wife? They were always there watching Colt's matches, their boy played.'

'I think I remember him, but I didn't watch many of the games last year, and when I did, it was usually only the first team matches. I caught bits of Colt's matches when they played on the pitch next to the first team pitch.'

'Bye-the-bye,' he hesitated, then - 'Well, it's Sam's wife Haley that needs some help.'

'Tell me more.'

Pete explained that he and Sam had become quite friendly over the last couple of seasons. In the closed season, they would also sometimes meet up for a beer and share the news.

'I was thinking of inviting him to join the '3C's' but never got around to it, and anyway, it all came to an end about three or four months ago when Sam, for some reason, no longer answered my text messages and seemed to have dropped out of the scene.' He added.

'Up until then, Sam and his wife Haley were always there at all of the Colt's home matches and had been 'regulars' at most social events at The Club. As I said, I tried to get in touch with him a few times recently, but Haley texted me to say he was away at the moment and that she would get him to contact me when he got back. I left it at that, I knew he was self-employed, and when you're in business for yourself, work has to take the lead.'

Pete explained that it was a mixed marriage. Sam was black, being of Afro-Caribbean lineage, and Haley white, and they had a young lad Rees who was about seventeen years old when Pete had seen them last.

'Sam didn't play at all. He loved the game, used to come up and watch all of the Colt's home matches, and told me that he had played himself when he was at school, loved the game, but had to give up playing after it was found that he had some sort of blood disorder - Sickle Cell disease or something like that. Listen, I don't really know much about what that all means, but I think he needed to be careful about anything that might lead to any sort of injury where he could end up needing blood. You'll need to talk with Haley, she will explain what it all means. I only know things second hand, but it's her that needs your help – it's something to do with Rees's health – I think he might need a kidney donation or something like that.'

'Well, I can't help with that,' I said, a poor attempt at hospital humour.

'Don't be a twat, you'll need to speak with Haley to get the full story, I don't know the details. She phoned me earlier this week asking if I knew anyone, from my old days in the police, someone private and discreet who might be able to help her sort out a serious problem that was breaking her up. I thought of you and Sally. You are still in the business of setting up some sort of private investigation thing, aren't you?'

I nodded, not that he could see me over the phone, but the silence he interpreted as my agreement with what he had just said.

'She asked me not to mention her call to Sam or Rees, as that would worry them and make matters worse, maybe get them into trouble. Listen, I don't know much more about this, just that it sounded like she was close to breaking point.'

'Okay,' I said. 'You've got my details. It's best if you ask Haley to get in touch with me direct. If I go calling her out of the blue, it might set things off on the wrong road. Ask her to give me a call, and I'll take it from there.'

'Thanks, mate – you're a gent, Chilli - even if you are a twat'.

That's what Rugger friends are for - people you can insult with impunity, without them taking offence.

Chapter 14 – Our First Client

Tuesday 17/1/23

I heard nothing from Haley until Tuesday the following week and was beginning to think it would all lead to nothing. Then halfway through the following Tuesday morning, I got a call on my mobile.

'Hello, can I speak with Mr. Pepper, please?'

It was a female voice, but not one I recognised. Whoever the caller was, she had to have known it was me, seeing as how she had just called my number, but I guess it was just good manners to verify my identity before continuing the conversation.

'Hi, that's me.'

'Hello, my name is Haley White - Pete Tanger said you might be able to help me?' Like most of Pete's close friends, she actually pronounced his name Tango.

'Hi Haley, yes he did say you might call. I'd be happy to help out if I can', I tried to keep the excitement out of my voice, 'It would be good if we could meet up in person, so I can get a better understanding of what the issue is and what assistance I might be able to provide. If I can help, I will, but I don't want to waste any of your time or create any false

138

hopes. Better if I know as much as possible about what help is needed from the outset.'

'Oh, that would be great if you could. I'm getting myself into a real tizzy – very upset, worrying about things. I just want someone I can talk to. Someone to make all of this go away.'

From the sound of her voice, it was apparent that she was on the verge of tears, and I needed to offer a little reassurance before it all got too much for her.

'Listen Haley, I can call you Haley, can't I? You can call me Chilli, everyone else does.'

'Yes, please call me Haley.' A long silence as I could hear her quietly sobbing. I sat quietly, just listening, waiting for her to find her own way of telling me and letting her compose herself in her own time.

'Sorry about that, it's all getting to me. I've felt like I have had no one to turn to.'

'Listen Haley, it's not good to try to do this over the phone. We need to meet up, so I can get a better picture of things, I understand it's about trying to find someone, or something, that has been lost, but I need some more information to help in the search, and I would like to bring along one of my colleagues with me so we can fully understand the problem and begin our search. My colleague has been involved in these sorts of searches before, and I'm sure she will be an asset in this instance.'

Haley sounded a bit hesitant, like she was undecided about something, but then told me that she was fine with this – she had picked up from what I had said that my colleague was a woman, and I got the impression that she was pleased - possibly even relieved - that a female Enquiry Agent was going to be involved in helping her. Maybe she thought it would be someone she could connect better with than a man. I was okay with that.

I didn't want to tell her we were, at present, not operating from any work-based offices or admit that we were currently working out of a garden room at the far end of my back lawn. Not that I was ashamed, I just felt it might put a bit of a dampener on things and wouldn't add much to her confidence in our ability to help.

So it was agreed we would meet up the following day at her house.

'I just need to check with my colleague Jules, but providing she is not tied up on another case, we could be at your place by, say, around 11 am?'

I assured her that if my colleague wasn't able to be there, not to worry, I would still come on my own anyway – I sensed Haley needed that assurance – it sounded like she was on the edge of things.

That was it – we were now 'officially' on our first real case. I just needed to speak with Julie to make sure she was available for tomorrow - that was a bit of a worry - and I had to let Mal and Sally know that things were kicking off.

Chapter 15 - A New Search

Tuesday 17th Jan - Early afternoon

That Tuesday afternoon rapidly became catch-back time. I had just made a commitment to meeting with our first client without making any of the proper sort of preparation necessary to ensure everything was properly prepared ahead of the game.

I had to make a fast recovery of the situation. I first checked my phone diary to make sure I wasn't expected elsewhere tomorrow. I was pretty certain that I was clear, but still a bit late in the day for doing that. All was okay there, thank God. I then called Jules to make sure she wasn't tied up with her ongoing NCA work or had any other personal commitments. Luck was on my side.

'So soon - Wow! There is nothing in my diary that can't be moved,' she told me, 'and I'm absolutely thrilled we are now on a real case all of our own.' The ball was rolling.

'Listen, Jules, she is not expecting to see us until 11 am. Why don't you drive over to my house first? Then we can both use my car to drive to Haley's. We can talk through how we are going to handle things when we are in the car.'

'Works for me, I can get there around 9 am if that's not too early?'

'No, make it 10 am, that will be fine. I have something I need to do earlier on.'

'Okay, 10 am it is.'

I took a few minutes to run through, in my mind, what had just taken place – time-wise I had been extremely lucky – I had made promises about being able to meet with Haley without checking with my diary or on Jules' availability first. That was an important and simple basic lesson I must and would learn from.

Jules, Mal, Sally, and I all needed a shared diary online. We all needed to be aware of each other's time commitments and movements to avoid any cockups in the future, cockups like the one I had just narrowly managed to avoid.

I didn't think we should take Mal along on this initial meeting with Haley and said so to Jules.

'Too many people there might intimidate her.'

'I agree, it would be a mistake to over-crowd Haley with people at this early stage and lessen our chances of picking up some pointers of where to start our search.'

'And Mal is better with the computer stuff,' she continued, 'we might need him with us at some time in the future, just so he can connect with things and feel more involved, but that can wait a bit.'

So that was how it began. Jules suggested she phone Mal to let him know that we had now officially started our first case, and as soon as things began to take shape and we needed to call on his expertise, he would be brought more into the thick of things.

'He's okay with that,' she told me later, 'he doesn't enjoy the groundwork side of investigations, too much like hard work, and he never had much of a liking for the people side of things. Tends to get a bit emotional. Bit of an old softy, really.' She added. 'Much prefers doing the online stuff, searching through the internet, and picking up leads that way. Sounds a bit weird to us simpletons, I suppose. Still, there's no accounting for taste.'

I was beginning to like Mal even more. It sounded like his preference for desktop work in our intended 'people tracking role' would fill an obvious gap in our preferred operating styles and so enhance the overall team capabilities.

When I arrived home, I grabbed her pink lead and poo bags and took Truffle out for her walk as a matter of priority. A nice long walk helped create a space for me to run through things and get some order in my thinking. I also took a break from the pent-up excitement that I was beginning to feel built up and used it as an opportunity to run through a few different possible approaches for our forthcoming meeting with Haley.

The fresh air not only benefited my thoughts, it also contributed to my 10,000 steps-a-day health target and, I told myself, help me maintain a modicum of fitness. It was also a promise I had made to Sally that I wouldn't let my newly found purpose in life interfere with my household chores and commitments.

So I ticked the box with my 'walkies' duty, then sorted the cats out with their afternoon feed and began to prepare a simple pasta meal for Sal and me, ready for when she got in. It wouldn't take more than 30 minutes to make and provided a bit of a much-needed distraction, so not really a chore.

Sally had been out at work all day and wasn't due back until after 5 pm. I checked the app on my phone to see that she had already left the college and was currently on her journey home. I timed my cooking to have the food ready, or nearly ready, for when she was due to arrive home and laid the table. Well trained, hey?

The tracking app was definitely one of the more useful apps on my phone. It tended to get more use the older I got, an invaluable way of finding where I had last left my car keys, my iPad, or tracking absent close family members.

When she got home, the food was on the table ready.

'You're getting good at this.' Sal told me. 'It tastes almost as good as it looks.'

'Almost a compliment,' I thought, 'she must have had a good day.'

Over our evening meal, we brought each other up to date with what had happened during our day so far. Sally was, of course, thrilled to hear that the Enquiry Agency was now starting out on its first real case! I told her about my talk with Haley and Jules and the simple and, in hindsight, very obvious lesson I had learnt about everyone needing to be aware of each other's location and availability constantly. Sally made the sensible link between my tracking her journey home so as to have her meal ready, with the advantage of always being able to locate each member of the team through the iPhone 'Find My' App.

'So sensible, you must all link up that way, you never know when it is likely to be needed.'

She was right, but I had already thought of that; of course, I just didn't want to mention it. I would need to check what type of mobile phone each of the others had though - it would be easy if we were all using iPhones, if not I didn't know what to do, so I made a mental note to ask Mal what might be needed to make it possible.

Sally and I talked through what other sorts of business challenges we might need to consider in terms of communicating with one another. Our new work role was not like a traditional office-based job where people generally worked together in a close vicinity and could be easily reached at any time. We needed to adapt, especially me, and make whatever fundamental changes were necessary to play by a different set of rules from what I had been accustomed to.

Sally was right, of course, but again I was already beginning to realise that myself, so she was only reinforcing the learning that experience had taught me some hours earlier. But that was fine with me; it helped drive it home. Linking up our phone diary calendars looked like another challenge best placed Mal's way.

I can't say I had a good night's sleep that night, my thoughts seemed to be racing around at 90 miles an hour.

'What if?' 'How should I?' 'What about?' - all going around and around in my mind. I think I finally fell asleep in the early hours, around what must have been 4 am. When Sal finally managed to wake me at 7:30 later that morning, I felt like someone had emptied a bucket of wet sand into my head.

It was a Wednesday morning, and Sally and I had a yoga class at the local fitness centre to go to first. That started at 9 am, and I didn't want to miss it if it could be helped, but I recognised that I would need to drop out after the first half an hour or so to get back in time for Jules. Also, the cats needed feeding and Truffle taken out for her morning walk, all before I could go 'charging off on my stallion to rescue the fair maid.' Sal, who shortened her yoga class at the same time to leave with me, thank heavens, came to my rescue.

'Don't worry about the animals, I'll take care of them, but I don't want this to become a habit.'

'Thanks a million, it won't, I promise.'

All of the time - my mind was elsewhere, already thinking ahead for the forthcoming meeting, playing possible scenarios through in my mind.

In hindsight, I thought I could have done with missing yoga this morning, but it was only a once-a-week commitment, and I would have to learn to take these new challenges on and find a better way of coping with my sleep if I was going to make things work. I would need to find some way of switching my anxiety off or at least tune it down a level or two. If I didn't, I wasn't going to last long in this business.

Then came my next major challenge of the day, what to wear for this inaugural meeting with our first prospective client? It may sound a bit daft, but what do private enquiry agents wear? I thought about asking Sal, but she wouldn't have known the answer any better than I would. I figured that the meeting location and the nature of the client would be the best-guiding factors. If our first client had been a business company or law firm, or if the meeting location had been so determined, then a smart business suit and tie would have been appropriate.

That wasn't to be the case here. Our prospective client was a distraught lady in her mid-thirties, with whom we were meeting in her own home. She would most likely be in need of some assurance that she was talking to people with whom she could most easily relate. A smart business suit and tie did not seem like it would be appropriate and might even restrict the working relationship we would need to establish from the outset. Again 'dressing down' too casually didn't seem right either, we had to give out the assurance that we were serious professionals, experienced in what we were doing. I searched through my wardrobe and settled for a casual paisley shirt, some navy-blue jeans, a brown check waistcoat that I had hardly ever worn previously, some tan brown leather walking shoes, and a casual tweed blazer jacket. Just a splash of aftershave over my beard. I thought, 'It all helps with the image.' Checked myself in the bathroom mirror, it felt right, and I was raring to go!

Could this be something of the 'Mal dress effect' beginning to have an influence on me?

Jules arrived at the stroke of 10. There was a light mist of rain in the air, but not enough to warrant the use of an umbrella.

Jules parked her little Smart Car on the road in front of my house and knocked loudly on our front door. I was ready for her and opened it before the door suffered too greatly from her assault. She bounced in through the opening as I held open the door for her. She was a sight to see, wearing a black beret, black leather gloves, her long black and grey plaid coat, and bright red lipstick emphasising her naturally pale complexion. I thought she bore a striking resemblance to one of the actors from the old 1980's 'Allo Allo' sitcom television series set in France during the last World War.

I was on the point of saying 'bonjour', but good sense prevailed. Not everyone appreciates my sense of humour so early in the morning, and there was always the danger that my unneeded remark might make Jules feel a little self-conscious. She was dressed for the part, and, in all honesty, what she was wearing looked good on her. ·

'Hi Chilli, Hi Sal - where-dat-wickle doggie?' she said as Truffle scampered up, rolling on her back for a tummy rub.

All a bit on the loud side of things for me this early in the morning, as I have already mentioned, I hadn't slept at all that well and had to struggle through the yoga class, finding it quite a challenge trying to achieve some of the bending and stretching positions others there, mainly women, seemed to bend into easily. Even I recognised that if I was to begin the banter too early on, I would be in danger of sounding like a moaning old git. So I took hold of myself and kept my comments to myself.

This wasn't the first time that Jules had met Truffle, but still that didn't matter to either of them, their mutual bonding was instant. Within seconds Truffle was swept up into Jules' arms and was trying excitedly to move her head around to a position where she could lick Julie's face.

'Cup of tea Jules?' Sal called out, 'You've got time if Chilli doesn't get lost trying to find the place.'

'I won't get lost, I used to live in Coventry, and anyway, I've got my Indian scout Tonto with me.'

'Yes, please, no sugar for me, please Sal – who's dis lubbly wickle doggie.'

'Righty-ho.' Sal called back from the kitchen, then 'And Chilli, don't forget to go to the toilet before you set off, you know what your bladder's like.'

'Great' - I thought, my self-image taking an unwelcome tumble from Sal's untimely reminder.

So that was that, we each hurriedly drank our cups of tea, eager to start our first case, just like a couple of kids again setting off on a new adventure.

'Shall we use your car or my Mercedes S-type?' Jules asked.

'Jules, much as I admire your tiny Smart Car, it would be a bit of a tight squeeze getting the both of us in it, and I think we might also make more of a favourable impression on our potential new client if we were to roll up in my Evoque.'

Jules smiled her acceptance of my logic, so we said our goodbyes to Sal and Truffle and set off for the Coundon district of Coventry, where Haley lived.

I knew the district quite well; it was where Coventry Rugby Club's pitch and clubhouse had once held residence before being relocated to their current location near the old Technical College on the edge of Earlsdon. I had visited Coundon Road many times during the 1970's to watch Coventry play and had been to one or two discos in the clubhouse there back in those days.

As we agreed we would, during the car journey Jules and I talked over what little we knew at this point in the case, not that we had much to go on at present. Summing it up, our assignment, which I figured would be relatively straightforward - though not necessarily easy - was to find a missing person or item and return them, or it, back to Haley where they, or it, belonged. It sounded like it was just the sort of thing we had planned on doing with our agency. But, as life teaches us, things are seldom that simple, certainly not in this new line of business.

We talked about how we would conduct the interview. Not much to say really, we both agreed I should take the lead as I had made that initial connection with Haley. That would leave Jules to observe any reactions or inflections I might miss.

'I'm going to refer to the whole thing as a 'search' when we talk to her. I don't want to call it an investigation, even though, of course, it will be. I just think calling it a 'search' will help keep the whole matter - at this stage - on an even keel. Agreed?'

'Yup - Agreed Kemosabe.'

We chatted about how things were starting to come together, and Jules told me that she had spoken with Mal, and when he got back from a prior appointment he had at the doctors, he was going to take a look through his internet channels to see if he could dig up any leads, anything at all on anyone called Sam, or Samuel White currently living in the Midlands area. The problem was White was a pretty common surname.

'He's not ill, is he? Mal, I mean - needing to go to the doctors?'

'No, he's okay. One thing I should tell you about Mal, now he's part of the team, is he is a bit of a hypochondriac, always dreaming he has some illness or other he has come across on the internet. It never amounts to anything. He finds mention of some sort of illness online, reads the symptoms - and thinks that he is suffering from them. I got used to him when we worked together in the police. There's sod-all wrong with him. Just an overactive imagination.'

'Fair enough,' I thought, 'I can live with that.'

'Just don't let him start talking to you about rare diseases - the day will pass you by.'

'Are you like 'Close' with him?' I asked.

She knew what I meant.

'Mind your own bloody business', I was told abruptly, but she smiled as she said it, and I thought I could see a sparkle in her eyes, so I sensed she wasn't offended by the question, and it didn't escape my attention that she never gave me an answer.

Chapter 16 - Haley's Story

Haley's house was a mid-terrace two-storey building, similar to my old house in Rothesay Avenue, and probably built around the same time, just after the Second World War. It seems like pebble dashing the front of the houses was the 'done thing' around that time.

A tiny front garden, with a patchwork of overly long grass and an assortment of weeds for a front lawn. And starring, as a prime attraction, two large black wheelie bins, one with a black lid and its companion with a blue lid. These shared most of the available garden space with an overgrown privet hedge, which served to help hold in place the remnants of a front fence, now partially buried within the hedge. The remnants of the garden gate were in pieces loosely hanging together and looking as if it had last served as a useful barrier some years back. The next most useful role this fence could serve would probably be as firewood. Still, we weren't there to do a critique of our prospective client's garden.

I noticed that there was no green-lidded bin there for the garden waste, which would have made up the full complement of bins, and assumed it was probably in the back garden where there would, in all likelihood, be another grassed lawn. Totally irrelevant, just me trying to string a few things together as a run-up ready for practising my investigative observational abilities.

I pressed the doorbell, but it made no sound; I tried again, no joy.

'Bloody hell.' Jules threw in. 'Give it a good knock.'

Smiling at her frustration, I used the metal letter flap, raising and letting it drop a few times to act as a door knocker.

We waited about ten seconds longer before hearing the sound of a safety chain rattling, and then the door opened. Staring back at us, half smiling, was a young lady that I had a vague recollection of having seen at some time previously. Probably, I would have come across her when I had, in earlier times, visited the Corley Rugby Club to watch one of the home matches.

'Hi - Mr. Pepper?' she asked.

'Yes, hi, and this is my colleague, Julie.'

'Jules, please call me Jules,' holding out her hand.

The lady, who we both correctly assumed to be Mrs. Haley White, lightly touched, rather than shook, first Julie's and then my hand.

We all put on our smiles of greeting and stood there a short while, each waiting for someone else to make the first move. I broke the impasse.

'Can we come in?' I asked.

'Oh, yes, of course, sorry - please do.'

There was an understandable hesitation of nervousness in her voice and in the way she looked at her two visitors, Jules and me.

We both, Jules and I that is, made a bit of a show of wiping our feet on the coir entrance matting in the porch area, even though we couldn't have picked up much dirt on the short path from my car to Haley's front door.

'Should we take off our shoes?' Jules asked.

I would never have thought of asking that. Wouldn't have been keen on the idea, a troublesome encumbrance, and, in truth, I couldn't remember what the state of repair my socks were in.

'Oh no, it will be alright, I will have to put the hoover around this afternoon anyway.'

She opened the door wider and stepped back, keeping a hold on the door catch until we passed through, then pushing it closed behind us.

'Please, please go on through. There's a fire in the back room.'

She waved us towards the second door down on the right, which was partially open and obviously the room where we were intended to go.

'Please, let me take your coats.'

We both shook off our coats, and Julie tucked her beret into her coat pocket before passing them to Haley, who hung them over the banister at the bottom of the stairs.

'Can I get you a cup of tea or a coffee?'

'That would be nice.' Jules piped in before I could answer. 'Coffee for both of us will be fine, black, no sugar, thanks.'

I didn't think either Jules or I were desperately in need of another hot drink, but it was a good 'icebreaker'. It also gave Haley space for a short distraction, allowing her to internalise the fact that we were actually there, and maybe help had arrived to help overcome her anxieties.

I took the opportunity to quietly glance around the hallway and begin to take in the surroundings as our first possible client guided us through into the back room. From what I could quickly observe, the inside of the house, unlike the garden, looked to be quite neat and tidy. Apparently, the vacuum cleaner and dust cloth had already been at work that morning prior to our arrival.

My first impression of Haley was that of a handsome lady, neatly dressed and in what I would assume to be her late thirties. With pale blue eyes, I guessed her fair hair colour was probably natural - not that it mattered, just practising my investigative skills again. Her hair was tied and gripped up in a bun high at the back of her head, a 'ready for business' style that, I guess, she felt best suited to the task in hand in a 'no nonsense' sort of way.

Dressed in faded loose-fitting blue jeans with a light grey polo-neck top that clung tightly to her upper body, the whole appearance served to emphasise her slight frame. She had, what I thought to be just a touch too much eye make-up, possibly applied in an unsuccessful manner to hide the obvious fact that she had recently been crying - not that I can claim any profound knowledge of what application of lady's mascara would be appropriate for an occasion like this.

Not visibly a great deal of jewellery, showing just a gold wristwatch and some large matching gold hoop earrings. I supposed, like Jules and I, she had dressed that morning with a need to feel comfortably smart and business-like, knowing she would be meeting with some new visitors for the first time.

'Please make yourselves comfortable; I'll be in in a minute.' We were told, as Haley made her way into the kitchen to make our coffees.

The back room, that we had now entered, was comfortably warm, the glow from the open coal fire being a welcome attraction.

Again, everything in this room looked like it had recently been tidied up in readiness for our visit. Nothing looked 'out of place', no newspapers or discarded clothing scattered around. There was one comfortable-looking and well-used armchair, embroidered with a green and brown flowery design of some sort, woven into its cloth covering and looking slightly sun faded on the one side closest to the back window.

The snagging of pulled threads on the side of the chair pointed to the presence of a cat and the chair's use as a claw scratch pad at some time in its history.

A small glass-topped coffee table with a Vogue magazine on it occupied the centre point between the seating and the television. Jules and I took to sharing the settee, which left the armchair for Haley to use when she returned with our coffees. That way, we would both be facing her directly when we finally got around to talking and allowing us both to observe her facial expressions and mannerisms as she talked.

I took out my mobile phone and placed it on the magazine, ready to record our conversation once we were all settled in and talking.

Haley came back into the room shortly after we had settled, carrying a small metal tray with three cups of black coffee, a saucer piled high with sugar lumps, and a small jug of warm milk. It was apparent everything had been already prepared prior to our arrival, the water in the kettle just needing to be reheated once we got there.

'Sorry, I can't remember. Did you say you wanted milk with your coffee?'

'No, thanks,' I cut in, 'We both take it black.'

We broke the ice quickly to get a conversation started, speaking about the change in the weather and the traffic, or lack of it, we had experienced on our journey over.

Then, bringing matters around to our purpose for being there. I touched my phone on the magazine, drawing Haley's attention to it.

'Haley, would you mind if I recorded our conversation? It's just that I want to make sure we capture everything relevant to the search, anything we may need to fall back on should there be any doubt on matters sometime later in our search. Please don't worry about it; we will erase anything not relevant once we have concluded the search.'

'That's okay, I don't have a problem with that. Just as long as you think it would help. But you have to promise that you will keep what I tell you a secret; otherwise, I don't know what I will do.'

Strange requirement, I thought, but Jules and I both nodded. We had no idea what we were about to hear, but Haley would now 'officially' be our client, providing, of course, all parties agreed, and once we knew what was required, that is.

I reiterated that we were new to the enquiry business but felt, with the skills we brought to the undertakings, we were well qualified to carry out our duties.

'Our prime focus is locating and, where appropriate, returning missing people or items to their rightful place. If, however, those people we searched for did not genuinely wish to be found, we were morally bound to comply with their wishes. We will only ever work within the bounds of the law, and I would make it clear that some of our team are still connected, as consultants, to the National Crime Agency.'

I felt that last bit, mentioning the NCA, probably gave us a little more credence than we deserved, it wasn't a lie, and why not use whatever aids we had if they served a useful purpose?

'As I mentioned, our enterprise is still in its infancy as a business, and as such, because we work as a not-for-profit business, we need to limit our searches and services to the West Midlands area.'

Haley nodded, gave what I felt to be a forced smile, and raised her hand briefly to indicate she was comfortable with the introductory explanation given, only asking for clarification on what the National Crime Agency was.

I let Jules take the stage on this, and she gave her well-practised short overview of the role of the NCA, 1 guessed it was an explanation she had had cause to do many times previously. She explained to Haley how the NCA was a relatively new policing service that had been formed back in 2013, working with regional police forces to combat serious crime that crossed over into different provincial areas of responsibility.

''The Press,' she told Haley, 'call the NCA the UK's equivalent of the USA's FBI. Maybe easiest to think of it that way.'

I could see that Haley was starting to look a little more hopeful that we might be able to help. However, I needed to add a little caution to what she was taking in. I didn't want to over-promise or give rise to any false hopes before we even knew what we were letting ourselves into.

'Haley, you have to understand that we are not the NCA, nor are we the police, we are a team of private enquiry agents who use our abilities in helping people find missing people. We do not have their resources in manpower or funding, so we need to look solely towards delivering those tasks that are within our capabilities.'

'I understand.' she said, nodding her head. I wasn't that sure that she really did, but let it ride.

One thing I did think, although I may have been imagining it, was that I was sensing what appeared to be something like relief in Haley's demeanour when I confirmed that we were not officially connected with the police.

I wondered if she really did understand what we could or couldn't do to help. I certainly hadn't wanted to undersell or overplay our capabilities, especially as we were still so raw ourselves at what we were doing. Those old seeds of doubt were still rattling around in my head!

But we were now in the race. No more time for hesitation. Now was the time to see if we really were up to putting things right and making a difference.

'What can you tell us about Sam's disappearance that we should need to know? Anything at all? We will see if we can piece it together once we have a better picture.'

Her body seemed to tense up, and I sensed a wariness in her attitude.

'Okay, but it's not really about Sam, and I don't want this to lead to him getting into trouble with the police; that is furthest from my mind', she said.

That stopped me in my tracks, I hadn't seen this coming - a big warning sign was flashing in the back of my mind. Only now was I beginning to sense that Jules and I had perhaps, been working under something of a misconception.

It appeared that we were only now starting to close on whatever it was that was causing Haley's distress.

'Don't worry about that. We are not here to sort out any associated crimes or issues like that. Our role is just to find Sam's location if he is missing and maybe, if he wants us to, get him to come out of hiding and make contact with you again.'

I still hadn't cottoned on to the fact that I, and I assume Julie, were approaching this investigation from completely the wrong avenue. Unwittingly, I ploughed ahead with my misdirected explanation.

'If we do come across anything serious, though, anything that needs police intervention, we will be obliged to notify them. You are our client, so, to the best of our abilities, we will be representing your interests throughout.'

I felt pretty pleased with the way in which I had given my explanation of our role and the limitations we were bound by. It seemed to satisfy Haley, and I sensed a release of tension in her body posture as she settled back to tell her story. At that point, I still hadn't realised that finding Sam was not at all the reason for Haley's worries. So still, I tumbled on, unaware of what we were about to be hit with.

'We will have the best chance of getting a result if we clearly understand what the problem is and are fully aware of all possible factors that may have a part to play in our search.'

Haley's expression had gradually changed during my explanation and had now taken on quite a worried look. I was only now starting to sense that there may possibly be some unspoken complications here and that things were not as they at first seemed.

Jules had picked up on this, too. She lifted her hand slightly to indicate she was about to speak.

'Haley, if we don't know everything, we are far less likely to be able to help. You have our promise that we will not be upset or judgemental about anything we hear, and our primary goal will be to help you through this difficult situation. But it is imperative that we go into our search knowing everything which could be a factor, whether you think it important or not.'

From the look on her face, there was an argument taking place in Haley's head, and that meant that there was definitely something we weren't being told.

She looked down, covering her eyes with one hand, like a child trying to hide herself.

'Okay, yes, I understand,' she said without looking up. Putting her coffee cup down onto the small glass-topped table, she brought both hands together, rubbing them nervously as if washing them without water, then dropping them into her lap. She looked up nervously to look into my face.

There was something that she was uncomfortable with obviously, but there was also now a look of defiance in her expression, a determination to finally get matters sorted.

'You have to promise that this will go no further,' her voice much stronger now than it had previously been, 'I must be able to trust you - Oh God - please understand. It's all my fault. I've been such a bloody fool. If only I could wind back the clock. If only.......'

She started to cry as she finally broke through her hesitancy to tell us her story; what little remaining mascara was now no more than round smudges that made it look like someone had bruised both of her eyes.

We let her tell her story without interruption, saving our questions until she had finished. I think both Jules and I sensed that if we interrupted the flow of Haley's monologue of what she considered to be her own failings, it would all fall apart and end in an incomprehensible diatribe of self-recrimination.

She told us her husband, Sam, wasn't missing at all. That had been just the story she had used to get Pete Tanger's help.

'Sam has his own window cleaning business. Not just one of the guys who do the 'household runs, he and his

167

regular team of cleaners have contracts with flats, housing associations, and office blocks all over. Mainly in the Midlands, but he has recently landed a few lucrative larger office contracts with clients as far apart as London and Manchester. Sometimes, if it was a large tower block job, for instance, that could mean him staying even longer away from home. If it is London or somewhere like that, he and his team might be away for anything up to a week.'

Most of his bigger jobs required him to work over the weekend. That made sense, I guessed, as that was when many offices with windows that needed cleaning were most likely to be closed or, at least, largely unoccupied over the weekends, allowing the cleaners greater access and less disturbance to the office workers when the cleaning was taking place.

When Sam was working away, Haley told us, she still went up to the Rugby Club to watch Rees play in the home matches. This had happened a couple of times prior to Christmas, and that was when she had begun to notice a man, who she had assumed to be another of the parents, always seemed to be looking her way.

'It wasn't just the once; I noticed it on a couple of occasions. If I looked back, he would smile and look down as if embarrassed.' Haley said, 'I didn't take too much notice.

I suppose I felt quite flattered that I was still able to turn a few heads.'

Shortly before Christmas, one of Haley's friends, Debora (Debby) Greenway had passed away. I had heard something about this from table talk at my last meal out with the Curry Club, but hadn't picked up on much of the detail.

'A sad story, so unexpected,' Haley said, 'Debby had taken her own life. Some sort of drug overdose. It was a tragic shock for Debby's family and friends. No one had spotted that Debby was at risk or needed support. There seemed no sense or reason for the suicide, and her son and husband are both still understandably in a state of shock. Debby's funeral was just before Christmas, a real dampener on Christmas celebrations for everyone who knew Debs.' She paused shortly as if to steady her thoughts, then, 'Half the Rugby Club at Corley, all those who had known Debby, attended her funeral, and everyone who turned up was invited back to the Clubhouse for sandwiches and a drink in remembrance of Debby's life. I had gone to the funeral with Melody, my friend. We had been pals with Debs since school days and had grown up with her. Our friendship had really grown when our boys had both joined the Colt's team a year or so back.'

She stopped for a few seconds, staring away, wiping her eyes, and blowing her nose into Jules' hanky.

Realising what she had done, she looked up at Jules and said, 'Oh my gosh, I'm sorry, it's your hanky, oh I'm so sorry.'

'Don't worry about it, just keep telling your story; the hanky doesn't matter.'

Her face reddened slightly with embarrassment, but she carried on with her story.

'Those of us who went back to the Corley Rugby Clubhouse for the - I suppose you would call it - the Wake.' She hesitated then. 'We were mainly the parents from the Colts team. Oh, there were a few of the older players with their wives, along with a mix of a few of Debby's friends from work. We all had a few drinks and talked about how shocked and saddened we all were. How could something like this happen to someone so young, still in the prime of her life, and without any of us noticing anything amiss?'

Later into the afternoon, the man, who Haley had noticed looking at her earlier, came over and introduced himself as Gary Goodfellow, he told Haley that he was one of the team coaches for Corley Colts and had been a friend of Debby's from way back.

'I didn't recall my son ever mentioning him, but maybe he had, and it hadn't registered with me without a face to put to the name.'

'He was a bit younger than me, nice looking - I had already had a few gin and tonics, and I guess I was quite open to the flattering advances of this new guy I'd met - it wasn't meant to lead to anything.'

She had assumed he was probably also the father of one of the other boys in Rees's team, as well as being a coach.

'He was different from most of the other guys in the Club. He was always dressed up quite fashionably when I'd seen him about before, smart jeans with a little turn-up at the bottom and a roll-neck jumper sort of bloke. Got the feeling he wasn't worried about what the other guys thought of him. Looked 'self-assured' - I suppose.'

She took a deep breath, then continued.

'He carried his phone, keys, and other stuff, I assume, in a leather shoulder bag, a 'man bag,' I think they're called. I guess it's a sensible place to keep your mobile if you don't have a coat on and don't want stuff sticking out of your trouser pockets. Anyway, it didn't seem to bother him. Just added to his image of self-assurance. I suppose the other guys had stopped taking the mickey out of him about it some time back when they could see he didn't react to their jibes.'

Over the course of the afternoon, Gary - who she thought looked a bit like 'Jack Sparrow' in the Pirates of the Caribbean films - insisted on buying Haley her drinks.

'I offered to pay my way, but he insisted he was 'a gentleman', and he said that if he continued buying me drinks, he could continue to enjoy my company. I was flattered and more than a little bit tipsy by then. Anyway, by the time everything was starting to wind down, it was late in the afternoon and beginning to get quite dark outside. Melody had already left; I was feeling more than a little inebriated and not relishing the thought of the walk back to the bus stop in the village.'

She wiped away some of her tears, smearing her eye makeup a little more. An unkind thought came to me that she would soon be looking like a panda if she didn't stop her tears soon. Not needed - and I immediately regretted thinking it.

Coincidently, as that rather unkind thought passed by me, Jules leaned over and handed Haley another white handkerchief. She must have carried a spare one in her shoulder bag.

'We were two of the last few remaining people in the Club by that time. I was in the 'land of the fairies' by then, I never was much good at holding my drink. This guy Gary seemed to still be coherent and sober. He said that I shouldn't try to walk back through the village to the bus stop alone and offered to give me a lift to my home in Coundon. I was surprised he knew where I lived, but figured I must have mentioned it.

Oh shit, what a fool I was, he must have been over the limit to drive, but I was past caring by then. Being driven home by a good-looking man, who just happened to look like Johnny Depp, seemed like a good idea.'

She started crying a little more intensely, wiping her tears and some more of her mascara away with Jule's hanky and further smearing the rest around her face.

'When we got home, he helped me to my door. I think he almost had to carry me. The drink must have well and truly hit me by then. He helped me into my house, Sam was away, and Rees was on a stay-over at a friend's.'

I don't, in all honesty, know what happened after we got inside. I think he gave me another drink that I seem to recall he it took from a hip flask that he had in that little brown leather satchel - the messenger bag thingy that he always carries, and that's all I can remember of the evening.

The next morning, I awoke in my bed with the most head-splitting hangover. My mouth tasted like I had swallowed a dustbin, and my clothes from the night before were scattered all over the room.

I remember thinking, you bloody fool, serves you right for drinking to the point of unconsciousness.

I had no idea of what was to come.

I showered and tried to tidy up my bedroom a little. I felt quite nauseous, and the thought of food was far from my mind, but I knew I must eat something to settle my tummy and managed to hold down a banana and a milky coffee.

The main living room was in a right shamble. Cushions were everywhere, and a white bed sheet that should have been in the airing cupboard was crumpled up on the floor. It looked like someone had rolled it up in a ball, and there were patches of what looked like baby oil all over it.'

She stopped for a moment as if rebalancing herself before continuing.

'I thought back to the shower I had taken when I first got up. I wasn't totally 'with it' at the time, but recalled that my skin had felt quite oily before the shower. It had to be connected. I'm not an idiot, I figured out what had happened: I had been taken advantage of sexually. I accepted that I had been a bloody fool but told myself I had no one to blame but myself.'

Another short spell of tears. Jules and I looked at one another, and Jules said, 'Haley, would you like to take a break for a few minutes? I could make a cup of tea for everyone while you regather your memories.'

'No, let me finish now I've started. If I don't speak it out now, I don't think I will ever be able to again. The worst is yet to come.'

We sat in silence for a minute or so as Haley gathered herself.

'I mean, he must have brought the baby oil with him in his bloody man bag. What sort of a sicko carries baby oil and things around with him when he goes to a funeral? He was all prepared and must have set out with the intention of doing this with some poor fool like me from the outset. His bloody man bag was his rape kit.'

She stood up and bent over to put a log on the fire, not that it needed it, but it gave her a distraction for a few seconds to allow her to gather herself again. She took a deep inhalation of breath and then told us.

'Later that afternoon, an email arrived from my new friend of the night before, Gary. How he had got my email address, I don't know, but anyway, it read;

'Hi beautiful, how was your head this morning? We had some fun, didn't we? Thought you might like the attached as a souvenir.'

'Oh God, it was disgusting - Attached,' she said, 'was the filthiest video of me being abused in the most terrible ways. He filmed me in every position imaginable. With his penis in my mouth and every other orifice, he could put it. He used

175

other things that were around the house to put into me. It was so dirty and sickening. I cried and cried for the rest of the day - the bastard, the dirty fucking bastard, how could he, how could anyone do that to me?'

Jules and I kept from saying anything. Again, it made sense to let Haley get it all off her chest and let her tell it in her own time and way.

'He used a banana to penetrate me - the one I had eaten for breakfast - Oh god - the bastard.'

I noticed that Jules and I both had instinctively glanced over towards the fruit bowl on the coffee table before looking down in an attempt to hide our involuntary reaction.

'And because he was holding the phone while he filmed it, he managed to keep his face out of the video. So there was no way of telling anyone watching it who it was using me in this way. It could have been anyone, but you could see it was a white guy, not my Sam.'

It was all quite sickening. I felt perhaps I should say something but reminded myself that it was best to remain silent and let Haley continue telling what had happened in her own way.

'Later that day, I got another email from the bastard. It said if I didn't want my husband and son to see what a friendly woman I was, I should consider joining his 'Health Club' for some personal fitness training. He said I could see in the video that I was in need of 'tightening up my abdominal muscles', but he would personally work on that with me. He would give me 'one-on-one' exercise lessons on a weekly basis, and for the first year, membership would be at half price. He made it obvious that this would not be a 'one-off' event! The bastard wanted to use me as his personal whore, and I was supposed to pay him for the privilege.'

Looking over at Jules, I could see that Haley's experience had hit her hard - this was not the sort of case that we had anticipated when the team had all agreed on the Ground Rules for our operation of the agency - searching for lost items or missing people.

'I wasn't going to let that 'shit' Goodfellow get away with it. I worried; oh God I worried, about what I was going to do. I decided that I wasn't the guilty party in this. He had to be made to pay for what he did to me.'

'So what was all of the blurb about Rees needing a kidney?' I asked.

'I'm so sorry about that, I am ashamed of that stupid story. It just came out when I was looking for what to do. It was sick, I know, but I wasn't in my right mind. I don't know how it all took hold; I hadn't planned on it all getting out of hand. I just needed something to tell 'Tango' to get his help, I knew he used to be in the police some years back, and I thought I could trust him to find someone to help me. I didn't know what to do; I'm ashamed of myself, I hadn't imagined it would grow out of control. Rees is not ill; he doesn't need a kidney. It's a wicked lie. I just started with that silly story, and it just grew out of control.'

She bent over, hiding her face in her hands, and we all sat there without speaking for a long moment.

I was trying to think of how I was going to tell Haley we would not be able to help. She had opened her heart out to us, and here I was, possibly looking at shutting the door on her.

Before I could find the words, Jules stepped in and took the wind out of my sails.

'Okay,' Jules said, 'if you want us to help you with this, we need to know the full truth. No more blind alleys, we have to know what it is we are getting into. Is anyone or anything missing? You know what our business is. What help exactly is it you are looking for from us?'

I wasn't sure I was following the direction Jules was taking this. It was beginning to sound like she had been won over into helping Haley, whatever the problem turned out to be. I had to play along.

Haley was looking distraught; she could see we were both trying to find what our role would be in helping her sort matters out.

'Can't you get him to give up the videos and leave me alone? I know he won't admit to having them, but anything, just anything to stop him, to make this go away.'

'Okay,' I said. 'We need to take this away and think through what we need to do to tackle the problem. What did you do with the email he sent you?'

'I deleted it. It was disgusting, I didn't want Sam or Rees to see it.'

'I know you said that you would tell Sam what had happened. Have you done so?'

'No, I couldn't; Sam would kill him. I wouldn't be able to stop him. I know that bastard deserves it, but I don't want Sam to do something that would land him in prison and all of this filth shared with the world. And it would destroy Rees. Oh God.' She was now bent over, holding her face in her hands.

I turned to Jules.

'I suppose it is far too late for Haley to have a rape test or to find whatever was used to drug her?' I said quietly.

'Afraid so', she said. 'You have to do that sort of testing as soon as you possibly can following the assault. He probably laced the alcohol he had in his hip flask with Rohypnol, or GHB, or something like that. Probably GHB, it also acts to lower inhibitions and make female users sexually aroused. But it is well-nigh impossible to trace that in the body this long after the event.'

'I wasn't sexually aroused.' Haley shouted. 'The bastard used me as a toy for his perversions!'

'No, no, I understand that. It would not be something you could have an influence on. You were raped, we fully understand. Please believe me. You have nothing to be ashamed of.'

There followed nearly a minute of silence while we all ran through the whole sorry situation in our heads.

Haley was crying in earnest now. I could see we would not be getting anything more lucid out of her at the present.

Then the voice of reason spoke through the dire gloom that seemed to have momentarily taken hold, and Jules brought us all back to earth.

She cut through the emotion, anger, and outrage that was cluttering my thinking and brought out the key factors that needed to be faced.

'We have to be very honest with ourselves here. We all accept that what Goodfellow has done is evil, and he deserves to be punished, but it is going to be something very difficult to be able to prove through a court of law. We believe, but cannot prove, that he spiked Haley's drink. His counterclaim would be that Haley had invited him into her house when her husband and son were away and that everything that followed was consensual. God - he could even claim that it had never happened at all. We have nothing, no evidence to prove matters one way or another.

Even if we had the disgusting video he took - which we don't - he could claim that it was Haley that came on to him and he was just complying with her wishes.'

She was right, and we, all three, knew it. The best that could be hoped for was that we could somehow get a hold of the original incriminating video together with any copies that might or might not exist and destroy them.

'Listen, Haley,' I said. 'We need to think this through to see what options we might be able to bring into being here. Can you keep it from Sam a while longer? A week, maybe? I accept that it will be difficult, but it would be good if we could come up with something that would allow us to nail this bastard without the need for anyone - and I'm thinking of Sam and Rees here, ending up in prison.'

Jules moved across to Haley and put her arm around her shoulders. Haley, still sobbing, nodded.

She sat there for a while, then.

'Rees will be the problem. Sam is away for the rest of the week, working down south. He won't be back until this time next week. Rees will be home from his friend's later today, but he spends most of his time when he's home, up in his

181

room playing computer games. I think I will be able to manage.

But I don't want to live with this, trying to hide it from Sam for the rest of my life. I've been a fool, but he doesn't deserve this. Sam is a good man, and something like this could 'send him off the rails.'

I nodded, there wasn't much more Jules or I could do without giving this whole matter some serious thought. I was also keen to get Mal and Sally involved to widen our thinking of possible approaches to the task at hand.

We stayed with Haley an hour or so longer, making sure we had all of the facts and digging into those areas where we needed clarification, then said our goodbyes, promising to keep Haley advised on a daily basis of how things were progressing.

The journey back to my house seemed inordinately long, and we travelled in near silence the whole way. The weather had cleared up a little, and Jules was driving as she had said, on the way over to Coventry, that she had always wanted to drive a Range Rover Evoque, so I had thrown her the keys for the drive back.

I had a few emails I wanted to type up and send, so it gave me the space to get things moving.

Both of us were running things through in our minds: the terrible story we had heard and possible approaches that we might be able to employ to address the problem.

'You realise that this is a long way away from what we all agreed would be our modus operandi when we agreed to go into finding missing people?' I said.

'Are you looking to backing out now?'

'No way, I'm in this all the way.'

'Me too, let's leave it at that.'

Whatever we came up with, I was determined this bastard Goodfellow needed to be taught a lesson he would never forget, and he had to pay for the grief he was causing.

Before we reached my home, I had 'Messaged' Mal, and it was agreed that he would meet us for a pow-wow at my house in an hour or so, later that afternoon.

Sal was at work at the college until 5 pm, so wouldn't be home until 6 pm when I would be able to fill her in on the problem and hopefully, by then, have a sensible plan of action we, the team, could put into play to sort matters out.

I also wanted to get some advice from Marcus, my youngest son, who currently works as a paralegal in Bristol while he finishes his studies and completed his training as a barrister.

I thought I knew the answers to what I was going to ask Marcus with regard to the chances of ever getting the slime-bag Goodfellow 'put away' for what he had and what he was still doing, but impartial free legal advice is as rare as 'rocking horse shit' and if you have an avenue for getting it, use it.

So I typed out a 'What if?' email to Marcus, giving him a general overview of the situation that Haley had found herself in and asking him for his opinion and any advice he may have to give. I knew he would be at work at the moment, so I wasn't expecting to get an answer from him until later that evening at the earliest.

Chapter 17 - What We Know and Don't Know

Early that Wednesday evening, I lit the old cast iron wood-coal burner in the front room of our house - I didn't want to use the Garden Room 'office'. It would take too long to heat the room up, and the ambience wasn't right somehow for trying to get our minds around the challenge Jules and I had just taken on.

I felt shattered, I don't know why, possibly just from listening to Haley's story, then the mental drain that followed as I tried to find some way through the maze.

The front room was cosy, especially so with the fire lit as it was now, and more the sort of place for us to clear our minds, ready to come up with a viable approach to employ in sorting this matter out. The only danger being that it was also somewhere, if I sat back to try to think things through in too much of a relaxed mood, I would need to take care not to drop off to sleep and embarrass myself in front of our newly formed team.

Certainly, a warm room, a comfortable chair, and a small group of people quietly playing out different scenarios in our minds was an open invitation to an old guy like me to doze off and take his afternoon nap. I struggled successfully to resist the urge.

Mal had turned up not long after we had arrived home and had settled himself on the old leather sofa, directly facing the wood burner. 'He'll cook there,' I thought, give it five minutes, and the heat will make it unbearable.

Jules had chosen the other chair by the window, and Truffle had commandeered Mal's lap as her temporary resting place.

We retold Haley's story to Mal.

I had early on recognised that Mal had a 'sensitive' nature about him and could see, from the expression on his face, that he was feeling quite unsettled by what he was hearing. I am pretty sure he would willingly want to participate in whatever action we felt necessary to sort matters out.

'What the hell is the world coming to when sicko's like this are about? This pervert needs to be taken down a peg or two. Shame she deleted the video', he said. 'I might have been able to trace it back somehow to get a clue as to what recording devices he used and where he might have it stored.'

'That's water under the bridge now,' Jules cut in. 'I'm pretty sure he would have just simply used his phone to record the whole thing. He probably wouldn't have thought to have stored it on any other device. He doesn't sound to me like he's the sort to get hung up on videoing techniques.'

'Yes, you're right, I suppose. I just wanted to have all the pieces of the jigsaw in place before we go making any wild assumptions.'

'We just might have to make a few assumptions here, we can never be totally sure we have everything, so let's start with what makes the most logical sense, not overcomplicating the problem.' I put in. 'Agreed?'

'Agreed', they both said, Mal perhaps a little more hesitantly, I could see he was still feeling a little uncomfortable with things as they stood.

'But you're right, Mal.' I chipped in. 'We need to have all of the pieces in the jigsaw first, or as many pieces as possible, before we make any wrong assumptions and go charging off in the wrong direction. Let's get the basics sorted first. Why don't I call out the tasks I think need addressing, and we each take ownership of those questions we think we are best suited to deal with most easily? And please - if anyone thinks of something I have missed, call out. You guys have years more experience in these sorts of case reviews than I do.'

'Sometimes it takes a fresh mind to break through the quagmire. We'll go with your approach, Chilli. Until I get bored with you taking the lead and send you off to make me another coffee.' Jules threw in.

'Good. Let's make a start. Where does Goodfellow live - his address? Where does he work? What is his prime source of income? Is he married? Kids? Where does he usually 'hang out' socially? Is he known to the police? Does he have a record?' 'What sorts of date rape drugs are there out there and how difficult is it to get a hold of them,' and so on.

We each threw in a few more questions, both Mal and Jules coming up with things I hadn't even thought of and possible routes we should explore further. It was a useful 'talk out' for each question or line of enquiry we felt we needed to look into. One of us would note it down in his or her small notebook, taking ownership of finding the answer.

I had bought similar notebooks for each of us that morning, insisting Jules stopped off at the local Sainsburys store on our way back from Haley's house. I'm sure both Jules and Mal would have been capable of providing their own notebooks. It was meant more as a gesture of us all being in the same team, a bit 'soft', I suppose, but it felt right at the time.

The notebooks were all of a similar design, but each had a different coloured wrap-around cover. Mine was black, Mal's navy blue, Sal's lime green, and Julie's pink. I had to admit there was a little 'of the devil' in me when choosing the pastel shades for the ladies. But my humour didn't go down too well with Jules, and after a little bit of sarcastic banter from her side of the room, I ended up with the pink book. It all amused Mal somewhat, but I could live with that.

Mal seemed to take ownership for most of the lines of enquiry, mainly because he claimed he could 'magic' out the missing answers from his computer.

Jules took on those tasks involving the need to access Goodfellow's police record.

'Don't land yourself in any trouble with your contacts within the police. We can't afford that.' I cautioned.

'Don't worry, she won't,' Mal remarked. 'But best if you just don't ask too many questions about how the answers she gets are achieved, though.'

He and Jules flashed a smile at one another, and I thought it best to leave it at that.

Whatever we did, we had to stay focused - trying to take on a problem, the magnitude of which might end up being beyond the capabilities of our little group of pensioners, would likely win us no friends. This was our first true commission, we couldn't afford to come up short, I needed to keep everyone focused on the challenge facing us immediately, that being to find the original and any copies of the video and destroy them. With that, we would be removing any hold that Gary Goodfellow might think he has over Haley.

Solving the growing problem of date rape crimes, or even punishing Goodfellow - while we all agreed he needed to be taught a lesson - was not something that we should be spending any of our time or resources on. If we could inflict some pain on Goodfellow when achieving our goal, but at no cost to our prime objective, it would, of course, be a welcome bonus.

I stressed this point to the rest of the team, and all agreed that it was essential we keep ourselves focused on the main task at hand. We talked away the rest of the afternoon, going over the situation time and time again, Mal feverishly tapping away at his MacBook computer throughout. We each suggested a few different possible scenarios and then shot them down whenever logic told us they wouldn't work.

Jules told us that she had encountered quite a number of date rape cases involving drink spiking while she was 'in uniform'.

'It's on the increase and never as simple as you would think to get a conviction for someone accused of rape or sexual assault,' She told us, 'There are currently over eighty-five thousand reported claims of rape, or sexual assault, a year in England and Wales. Only one in a hundred result in someone being charged and taken to court, and of those that do get to court, only seventy percent finally lead to a conviction.'

'Some types of date rape drugs like GHB are particularly nasty,' she added, 'They work with the alcohol consumed to lower the natural inhibitions of the person targeted with them, resulting in female users often becoming sexually aroused and behaving in an uncharacteristically flirtatious manner. If they do remember what has happened, they often assume that they were equally responsible for the resulting sexual infringement.'

'Sounds like that could be whatever Goodfellow used on Haley.' I said.

'It's worse than that in reality.' Jules added. 'Those with experience in this sort of crime estimate that the stigma and self-shame that victims feel they have to face in making such a rape claim result in five out of six women who have suffered this sort of thing not reporting the crime to the authorities.'

That did little to inspire our confidence in finding a solution and getting the matter sorted out through the appropriate channels.

Sally joined us as soon as she got home. She was happy with her lime green notebook, no worries about the colour, just felt it would have been better if I had splashed out a bit more of my pension and chosen some more expensive ones which would have come with their own pencils and rubbers. She, of course, made her observations out loud to everyone present.

She was right, of course.

We brought her up to speed with the happenings of the day and the tasks each of us had agreed to take on from this point moving forward.

Sally also came good in our subsequent discussions. She provided the 'level head' that kept us focused on what needed to be done and checked us, noticeably me when we wandered off into what was just fanciful thinking.

'So, it's 'Round One' then, and already you have decided to take on a problem that only holds a loose alliance to the Ground Rules we all jointly agreed on?'

She was right, and the room fell into silence for an awkward second or two. Then Sal shrugged and said.

'I think, in this instance, you are right. If anything needs settling, it's this. Have you decided what you are going to do?' She was looking straight at me.

'No, not really, the only thing we all agree on is the need to locate all of the copies of the video and destroy them.'

'Right - and how are you going to go about that? Do you need to get access to his phone and computer?'

'Yup.'

'Right, so what's the plan?'

She had the knack of cutting straight to the point.

'Well, my thinking is that we need to grab his mobile phone and any computers he may have. Then wipe them.'

'That's what I just said!'

'Yup.'

Mal looked up and smiled.

'Not necessarily. Either his phone or computer will do,' he said. 'But, if you can get a hold of either one, computer or phone, I can probably find a way of installing some malware, a 'worm' probably, something that can be the pathway into all of the other stuff he has in his files. I can programme the 'worm' to clean out the software memories from any other computer or phone that happens to try to link up with it. That way, if he has already shared it with anyone, then when they try to access the material in the future, the 'worm' will clean out their file.'

'You can see why they call him 'Malware'.' Jules threw in.

'Brilliant, then that sounds like it has to be the focus of our attentional.' said Sal, as if it was just as easy as that.

'Ideally yes, you're right. Both computer and phone,' Mal replied. 'But, failing that one or the other.'

'Yup.' - My contribution to any conversation that touched on computer technology served to demonstrate my discomfort. Trojan viruses and planting 'worms' were something that far outstretched my understanding. Still, I got the gist.

After another hour or so, again just talking around what could be done and getting nowhere, I suggested that everyone needed to take 'time-out' to do a few of the other tasks we had set ourselves and clear our heads a little. Hopefully, we might then be in a better place to let new thoughts and ideas emerge and begin to plan our way forward.

It was agreed that we all would take the problem and any of our allotted tasks away with us, sleep on it, and see what fresh ideas might emerge. We could all then also do a little research of our own, the following morning, and share our progress when we met up later that day.

My suggestion was that we leave it until early in the afternoon tomorrow, after lunch. I wasn't into making lunch for everyone; they could make their own lunch and use the drive-over to my house to 'limber up' for the afternoon's information sharing and group 'brainstorming'.

This time, it was agreed we would use the garden room, map out the critical points and the answers found so far - using Sharpies and Post-It notes - on the wall as a means of recording our findings and hopefully it might point us towards the way forward.

I made a mental note to remember to switch the small electric heater in the garden room tomorrow morning.

We really needed an office somewhere. Somewhere where I could fix a large whiteboard to the wall and track progress with a non-permanent marker pen. Like the police do in all of the crime dramas on the TV. But that was dreaming ahead, and I lightly chided myself. This was, after all, our first commission, and we needed to prove ourselves capable before planning out new office accommodation.

I had a few other things - household chores that wanted doing before then, and I needed to try to clear the whole thing out of my mind for a spell, just an hour or so, then come back to it afresh, maybe take Truffle out for a long walk or something. That was the best way for me to work; I found that new ideas quite often emerge when you put the problem to the back of your mind for a short while.

I knew Mal and Jules would be beavering away as soon as they got home, digging into the background questions that we needed answers to, so that we would have something to work from and be able to take matters forwards.

Marcus, my son, the barrister, came back to me with a response to the email I had sent him earlier in the day with answers to my questions on the 'legal position' regarding the situation we were in with Haley.

His response read; 'I'd say they would be unlikely to prosecute based on the evidence your client can provide. And, you have the possibility that, even if the video still existed, it might, even then, not be admissible.'

The reason for that being that if the video is as disturbing as you say it is but does not show clearly that the man you suspect to be the perpetrator actually is the person carrying out the crime, it will run the risk of having an adverse effect on the fairness of proceedings.

The Defence team would object to the showing of the video, claiming it would be prejudicing the jury - without proof that it's the accused person involved in the actual rape.

If he's trying to blackmail her with the video, that means he still has possession of the video. If she told police that she was being blackmailed and if there was evidence of that, which could be shown, you might have something to go on.

Or if the police raided and seized this person's belongings and found the video or some other documentary evidence, it would be difficult not to draw an adverse inference without a credible explanation. Especially when you have a video of someone being raped (not to mention the multiple criminal acts involved in possessing that in the first place) and proof that he took the video and that it is him in the video.'

A convoluted reply, but as expected, Marcus's guidance only served to confirm what our small team had already surmised; it was extremely unlikely that we would be able to resolve Haley's problem by trying to go through the proper legal channels. Solving this would need a slightly more indirect approach. More like a 'vigilante approach'.

It all boiled down to the fact that we needed Goodfellow's phone and, I guess, his password or whatever was also needed to access what was stored on his phone.

-0-0-0-

Mid-morning the following day, we met up again. All in all, the team had 'come up trumps' with answers to most of the questions we had shared out the day before, and gradually, a picture of Gary Goodfellow - began to take shape. We now had a better understanding of who our adversary was, where he lived, what he did for a living, etc.

I had spoken with Pete Tanger again, and he added to the picture we were building of Goodfellow. Pete told me he had been out for a drink with a couple of the lads from the old team last night and had asked them about what they knew of Goodfellow.

'Neither of the guys I spoke with, Brent Grant and Ivor Williams, had a good word to say about Goodfellow. Seems he never went out of his way to build up many friends.'

Goodfellow apparently had played for Corley Rugby Club about ten years back while his dad, my old adversary, was still alive, but he had given up playing after a minor injury to his leg, twisted his knee, or something like that. It was at the time when I was living and working in South Africa with my previous job, so that explained why I hadn't come across him before.

'He wasn't a very good player, too worried about getting his shorts muddy.' Pete Tanger had told me.

I also learned from Pete that Goodfellow was - he thought - an 'only child', had got divorced about seven years back, had no known children, to the best of anyone's knowledge, and didn't have a regular girlfriend. Word was that the few women whom Goodfellow had shared a relationship with over the years didn't seem to want to stay with him for long.

'More like one-night-stands than anything more lasting seems to be the shape of things. Whether that was by choice or not, no one seemed to know. Rumour was he had been a little on the rough side with one of the girls in the village some time back, but her brothers had stepped in and warned him off. Just a rumour, but I wouldn't put it past him.'

Pete added that he knew that some of the ladies up at the Club had indicated that they didn't feel comfortable with Goodfellow coaching their sons.

'Nothing they could put into words, just an uncomfortable feeling they had about him!'

Goodfellow ran his own business, a private gym that he preferred to call a 'fitness centre' on the outskirts of Bedworth. Pete went on to tell me that, while he hadn't been there himself, the gym was allegedly a scruffy place. Most of the equipment there is second-hand recycled stuff scavenged from other gyms that had ceased operating or from other more established gyms that had 'sold on' their old equipment as it needed renewing over the years.

'I'm told it is mostly a collection of old 'traditional' fitness equipment and an assortment of weights, Indian clubs, medicine balls, skipping ropes, and tatty workout mats. I had thought about taking a look at joining sometime back but decided it was not worth taking out a year's membership. I've heard he's now got a couple of cycling machines and a rower and a few other gadgets, but nothing too clever.'

'The building itself was once an old Barclays Bank that had been converted into the gym on the ground-floor level with living quarters up on the first floor, where the old management offices used to be. That's where Goodfellow lives, up above the gym. Why all of the interest in that scumbag? I thought you were working for Haley and on the trail of Sam?' Pete asked, understandably wondering why I was pumping him for information about Goodfellow, not Sam.

'Can't tell you anything at the moment Pete, just a line I am working on. It might be nothing. I'll fill in with all of the background, or what I can at least, when we have our next Curry Night.'

'I'll hold you to that.'

He would, too, I would need to concoct a well-prepared tale ready for when we met up again.

'Listen Chilli,' he threw in, 'I thought you were in this to help Haley out, you better not be tugging my chain on this. I used to be a close friend with Sam and Haley.'

'I'm not Pete, you have my word on that and I am working for Haley on this. I will fill you in with as much as I am able to when we meet. But you have to remember that I have a responsibility to maintain client confidentiality if I am to operate effectively.'

He seemed to accept this, at least for the time being, as he had come across similar sorts of reservations and limitations from outside parties during his years in the Police Force.

From Pete, I also learned that Goodfellow spent most of his working days, 9am to 5pm, during the week, in his fitness centre. Unusual, I thought, unless he had some other source of attracting clients for his centre, I would have expected his busiest gym times would be during the early evening, the after-work hours, and, of course, at weekends. So what business was keeping him busy and tied to the fitness centre during the working day?

'I've heard that when he's not flitting about up at the Rugby Club, he's working out in his gym. Fancies himself as a bit of a lady's man. Calls himself the 'Tooth Fairy', supposed to frighten people who get on his wrong side.' Pete said. 'His pal Barry Spencer, or 'Blow Torch', as the twat likes to be called, is his only employee.'

Another short snort of laughter then; 'I've heard a bit of speculation by some of the guys in the Curry Club about the type of relationship between Goodfellow and Spencer, but nobody really knew anything. But that's just talk. Some of the guys will hang any sort of tag they can think of on people they don't care for.

Blow Torch' and 'The Tooth Fairy' - Barry and Gary - I ask you, what the bloody hell is the world coming to?' He gave another snort of a laugh. 'Spencer apparently works for

Goodfellow as a 'fitness trainer' - come, receptionist - come hygiene specialist. What Goodfellow actually does there and what purpose he serves, I have no idea. I think he just likes to lord it around as 'the boss'.

He gave another of his snorting laughs then - 'Word is that he has a room overlooking the fitness centre in one of the old offices there above the weights-room, or walking around smiling at the gym users, especially the ladies.'

'You're a star, Pete; if you ever think of moving over into the Private Enquiry side of things, let me know.'

'You've got to be bloody joking. I hung up my helmet and truncheon many years ago; too much hassle, and, if I hear right, you are doing this work for free - no way.'

I thanked Pete for his help and once again promised to buy him a pint when we next met up and to bring him up to speed with things once we had matters sorted.

I slipped the phone back into my shirt pocket and sat back for a few seconds absorbing what I had learnt, then summarised the information Pete had given me with the rest of the team. I gave them a minute or so just to let them think through what we had just learned, before breaking into the silence.

'Listen,' I said, 'This guy Goodfellow doesn't know me, or at least doesn't know me well. I've been thinking, why don't I go over to Goodfellow's place on the pretext of taking out a temporary membership in his fitness centre, whatever the shortest period is to sign up for? That way, I might be able to see what 'computer type' devices he has use of and maybe see if I can learn anything from Spencer, this 'Blowwave' guy. Can't do much harm, and it at least gets us closer to the action.'

'I don't know about that.' Sally said warily.

'Whoa, whoa, Kemosabe.' Jules threw in. 'You don't know what you might be walking into.'

'Anyone else got a better idea?'

'Yes,' Jules said, 'I should be the one to join the fitness centre. We know Goodfellow has an eye for the ladies. I might not be a spring chicken, but when I'm in my leotard, I can still turn a few heads.'

'We could both go together,' said Sally, 'two ladies, a much safer way of carrying out surveillance.'

'Look,' I said. 'I'm not happy with anyone putting themselves in harm's way, and I think the two of you joining his gym might be a good thing for us to consider as things progress. But this will just be a scouting trip, and I want to get a handle on Goodfellow myself before we take things any further. So, it will be me who visits Goodfellow's gym. I don't have to join. If that's what's worrying everyone, I'll just call in and make a few enquiries about membership. Let's leave it at that. We'll get nowhere if we sit on the side

203

of this problem arguing about who does what without engaging with the issues.'

Everyone knew I was right - they might not have liked it - but I gave them no time to think up other objections. What choices were there? What had to be, had to be. And that was where we left it.

Chapter 18 - Locked Out

Friday 3rd/2 - Morning

Early the next morning, I drove over to Bedworth, to the address Pete Tanger had given me for 'Goodfellow's Fitness Centre'.

I got there about nine in the morning, taking my kit bag with me, just in case things moved that way, but as 'sod's law' would have it, the Centre was closed. No lights on in the building. Well, it was morning, so maybe they weren't needed? But there were no notices, or anything, on the doors or on the outside of the building itself, to show what the 'opening times' were. Being an old bank, the windows were of frosted glass, so it was impossible to see through them and into the building itself. I had looked the place up on Google last night and saw that the gym should have opened at 6:30 this morning. It was now 9:15. I checked with Google again on my phone, just to make sure I had got it right and to see if maybe anything had been posted to say why it wasn't open; there was no updated explanation there.

On my drive in, I noticed a small 'One Stop' shop on the corner of the road, just two buildings down from the gym, so I walked down and called in to ask if they knew why the fitness centre/gym was closed. The lady working behind the counter was probably about my age, but time had not been too kind with her health. She was using the aid of a walking stick to help her make her way around the shop, and it was difficult to imagine how she managed to keep the shelves stocked up. She probably had someone who came in to help her with tasks like that, I thought.

'Excuse me; I was wondering if you could help me?' I asked, smiling and putting on, what I thought to be, a 'worried I'm lost' expression on my face. 'Do you happen to know at what time the fitness centre, two doors down, opens?'

'I wouldn't know luv. They're a bloody law unto themselves there. Sometimes open until late at night, sometimes closed for days at a time. It's a wonder they do any business at all. The times I've seen people turn up there only to walk away because the bloody place is closed. That's not how to run a bloody business!'

I thanked her, went back to the Centre, and thumped on the door for a few moments. Then, a voice called out from an upstairs window.

'Piss off. I'm busy.' A bloke's voice, but I could hear the faint sound of a female giggling in the background. Apparently, I was interrupting something. Not quite what I was expecting, I must admit. This guy lacked some basic business and customer-handling skills.

I wasn't much into sharing my business with the whole neighbourhood by holding a 'pavement to upstairs window' shouting conversation, but this guy had seriously got my back up, so I responded in kind.

'It's Chilli Pepper from the Corley Rugger Club,' I shouted, 'I was looking at maybe joining the fitness centre - if it's not too much trouble.' Mild sarcasm leaching into my response there.

'Leave me your number, I'll give you a call when I'm up,' the female laughter coming through again. She mumbled something, and I heard him laugh as well.

'Look, Mr. Pepper, I'm a bit tied up at the moment. I'll sort out some special terms for you if you're interested in joining. I remember you. You used to be a pal of my dad's in the old days, weren't you? I recall him saying, years back, that he owed you one. Can't talk at present, doing some one-on-one personal training. Give me an hour or two, I promise I'll get back to you later this morning.'

His dad 'owed me one?' - he probably did, I thought, 'but not in the way you think'.

The devil was in me - 'Upset my morning, will you, you bastard?' I thought.

'Okay,' I shouted, 'It was Haley White who recommended you and said you were cheap.'

No reply - but the silence was 'audible', if such a thing was possible, and the window was slammed shut.

Well, that was that, I wasn't going to get anywhere here this morning. One more reason, to add to all the others, for me disliking this joker.

I didn't get to meet Goodfellow, as was my intention, and didn't get to see inside his gym. I had no idea what computers or other devices he might own. So far, the day had been a complete write-off. Not a great start to my investigation. I had a few other things to do; otherwise, it would have been just a wasted morning.

Nothing much further happened in 'the way of progress' on our first case that day. Each of the 'Sap-laf-fea team' worked on whatever we had agreed were our own tasks in building as complete a picture as we possibly could of Gary Goodfellow and his pal Barry Spencer.

Chapter 19- A Carpark Encounter

Saturday 4th/2 Morning

Early the next day, shortly after the store had opened, I was standing in the local Sainsbury's car park where I had just completed my week's top-up shop. It hadn't taken long, mainly just a few things I had forgotten to get when I had done the main shop a week or so before. It was a damp morning, but the drizzle had eased up a little.

It was a quick shop, not too many people about that early on a Saturday morning. I had been lifting my carrier bag of groceries into the Evoque's rear luggage area, and as I pressed the button underneath the up-and-over door, something or someone gave me an almighty push, knocking my head against the bottom of the descending door.

The sensor on the door registered that there had been an obstruction, my forehead, and stopped its motion downwards. I fell forwards into the luggage space area, both hands reaching forwards to halt my fall. My right hand landed within a couple of inches of the leadwood stool leg I kept there. On impulse, I grabbed it and swung the heavy wooden club in an arc back towards where I had just, seconds before, been standing.

The wood connected with a juddering thwack against something hard, which turned out to be the left ear and side of someone's head. It was a complete stranger, and for a split second, I felt a brief worry that I had just struck someone who had innocently bumped into me.

The man I had struck had fallen to his knees and was clutching his ear and the side of his head, moaning.

'I'm sorry, I'm sorry,' he cried, 'Not supposed to happen, just wanted to scare you. I'm hurt, I think you've cracked my skull.'

A bald-headed man, who looked to be in his mid-forties, was kneeling in a puddle on the car park asphalt in front of me. Dressed in a Denim jacket and jeans, artificially torn at the knees, a style more suited I felt for a much younger person. And - 'double Denim' - my daughter would not have been impressed with this guy's dress sense.

He looked like he would be an inch or two taller than me if he was standing. But it was more difficult to judge his height as, at that moment, he was still down on both knees, kneeling in a rainwater puddle on the car park's tarred surface.

I realised what had happened, I had the gods on my side again. After shoving me into the closing tailgate of my car, he had taken a quick glance around to make sure no one in the car park was looking our way. It would have cost him maybe a second or two in time, but long enough for me to grab my stool leg and spin, clobbering him before he could put, whatever his next plan was to do, into practice.

I could see he was one of those guys who felt the need to decorate his neck and head with an arraignment of black and grey tattoos. There was now a good splash of red, adding colour to the left-hand side of his head and obscuring whatever the tattoos there were supposed to be. The red was from the blood that was now beginning to flow liberally from the split in his ear lobe. It would probably need a stitch or two to fix, but that would be his problem, not mine.

From the lack of focus in his eyes, he was also going to have quite a headache for some time to come. It could be a little concussion that might result from his encounter with a piece of South African leadwood, another reason for a trip to A & E for him.

I looked around the carpark, and there were only one or two people on the far side loading groceries into their cars. No one seemed to have registered the incident.

'Right, you shite, what the fuck is going on?' I let him see the stool leg in my hand, ready to strike again if necessary.

'Nothing, I promise, it was just an accident. A joke. I didn't mean to bump you.'

'Bullshit, you just told me you were out to scare me. Tell me what this is all about, or you will need to explain at the hospital how you managed to split both ears.'

'It's just this ear,' he said.

I lifted the stool leg and moved towards him.

'No, no, I see what you mean, sorry, sorry Mr Pepper.'

This clown's not the brightest of sparks, I thought. It was no accident; he knew my name, and he knew what he was doing when he came after me.

'So you know my name. Who the fuck are you? And don't give me no shit.'

'I'm Barry - Barry Spencer, a friend of Gary Goodfellow - the 'Tooth Fairy.'

He stopped talking and looked up, as best as he was able, trying to see if his words would have some sort of impact, but I didn't let it show that it meant anything to me.

'So, who is this Poof Fairy?' Sounds like he's your boyfriend, the way you expect me to start quivering at the sound of his name.'

I made out that I had never heard of anyone called the 'Tooth Fairy. I didn't want this twat thinking the name meant anything to me. I had to try and pry everything I could from this joker while I had the opportunity. Starting with why the sod had attacked me.

I could see that he was actually starting to cry, a real flood of tears running down his cheeks. I wasn't sure if this was a by-product of concussion or not, but I couldn't feel any sorrow for him. He'd brought it on himself.

Still, I found it difficult to stay too rigid when seeing a grown man, even this git, crying like a baby.

Remembering what Sal had said about taking as many pictures as possible 'Just in case,' I took out my phone and snapped some shots of the clown on his knees bleeding and blubbering, the carpark, and a self-portrait of myself showing the tiny scrape, blood and all, on my forehead just below my hairline.

'Has this got anything to do with Sam and Haley White?' No medals for guessing that given that it was the one and only missing person case my friends and I were currently involved with, and given that I had just, earlier the previous morning, made an unsuccessful visit to meet up with his boss. I thought it highly likely. Call it an Enquiry Agent's intuition.

He didn't reply, but I could see my supposition had struck home.

'Listen, you little shite.'

Calling him 'little' was just a turn of phrase, as I figured that, if not kneeling as he currently was, he was probably as tall, maybe slightly taller than me. That would have made him around the six-foot mark when standing, which, at that moment, he was decidedly incapable of doing.

'If this Poof Fairy' - (deliberately getting the name wrong again in a school-yard attempt to show I wasn't impressed with the silly name) - 'wants to talk with me, I'm happy to oblige - I'll even make the effort and travel over to Bedworth again, I want to see inside his gym and then have a civilised conversation without any of this sort of shite. The meeting will take place this week - in the daylight - where little shites like you can't sneak up on me from behind. Make sure you tell him that.'

'Yes, I'll tell him - civilised conversation.'

'You've got it.'

I pulled out my wallet and took one of our newly printed business cards, with mine and Julie's phone numbers on, and stuffed it unceremoniously into the top pocket of his Denham jacket.

I hadn't yet gotten around to adding Mal's phone number to the cards; he having joined us after I had already commissioned the cards for Jules and myself and wasn't going to waste the ones we had already printed. Mal could always be added later, once I was sure he was going to stick around with us and also when we had used most of the ones already printed, and it became time for a reprint. Not that I keep a padlock on my wallet, it's just, being of Welsh lineage, I share their trait of not needlessly wasting money.

'That's my phone number.' I told him. 'And I'm going to make sure a few people I know learn about this and that you and your friend the Poof Fairy are involved. Then if you ever try any of this sort of shit again, they will know on whose door to knock. You understand?'

'Yeah, yeah, fully understood, sorry Mr Pepper.'

'And stop saying sorry, you twat.'

I helped him up onto his feet, using my left hand and arm and keeping my right arm, with the stool leg, free just in case the dazed awkwardness he was portraying was an act. He didn't try anything, and I figured he definitely still wasn't compos mentis.

'Where's your car?' I asked.

'Over there,' he said, waving his arm loosely in the general direction of the far side of the car park.

'Bugger that, you're too dazed to drive.'

He didn't argue, and I half-carried/half-walked him over to the passenger side-door of my car and helped him in.

'Where's your keys?' I asked. He put his hand in his pocket - I watched him carefully - and pulled out a set of keys and handed them to me. Not the slightest sign of resistance in his actions now.

I threw them into the long grass at the side of the car park.

'Can't have you thinking I'm getting soft.' I said. 'They will be safe there. You will have to look for them when you get out of hospital.'

I told him to belt up and keep leant over to the right-hand side so that the blood from his ear lobe did not get onto my car seats. He looked a bloody mess; tears and blood had mingled and soaked the collar of his shirt and denim jacket, and mucus was dribbling from both nostrils.

I had to help him fasten his seatbelt before I got in my side of the car. Then, I drove him the three or four miles to the entrance by the A & E department at Warwick Hospital. He was quiet the whole journey, and as I had nothing more to ask at the moment, we journeyed the whole way without saying another word.

As fate would have it, the sound system in my car had tuned itself into Spotify and was playing 'No Regrets,' the original Walker Brothers version. I could see out of the corner of my eye that Spencer's mouth was moving as he sang along in silence. I guessed it was a sensible move of mine to drive him to A & E; the guy was definitely doolally from his head injury.

The journey was uneventful, and once we arrived at the 'short stay - drop off' area of the hospital, I pulled in, got out of the driving seat, and walked around to open the passenger side door. I unfastened his seat belt, helped him to his feet and pointed him at the main doorway before letting him find his own way across the hospital carpark into the A&E entrance. There, I left him to get his check-up, stitches in his ear lobe, and whatever other help he might need, got back into my car, and drove out before having to pay for a parking space.

I figured he would be able to make up whatever story he liked to explain how his injury had occurred, no doubt whatever he fabricated for the medical staff would be a complete pile of bullshit.

The throwaway comment I made to Goodfellow when I visited his gym about Haley saying he was 'cheap' had, it would appear, been the catalyst for the unsuccessful car park attack on me by Spencer. It was safe to assume that I had stirred up a hornet's nest and this twat Goodfellow was trying to warn me to keep my nose out of his affairs and hoping to scare me off. He'd have another think coming.

I made my way back home, using the journey to try to get things sorted into the right order in my mind.

I was annoyed with myself, I had been bloody stupid in mentioning Haley's name when I visited Goodfellow's gym. That had brought about the subsequent bit of bother in the carpark and had probably now blown any chances I may have had of getting into the gym for a look around.

Chapter 20 - Setting Things Straight

Saturday 4th/2 pm

I decided not to make too much of the car park incident when I spoke with Sally. I didn't want to worry her unnecessarily, and it was too soon to pull the rug out from under our inquiry, something which I was sure she would insist on if she thought we were in over our heads and that someone might likely get hurt as a result. But I couldn't hide the tiny scuff on my forehead where I had banged my head on the rear door of the car, so the safest course of action was to just make light of the incident.

I explained to Sal that someone had bumped into me while I was loading the groceries into the tailgate area, and I had caught my head on the door. It wasn't a lie, but not strictly the out-and-out truth either.

I got the sympathy I deserved.

'You're not getting any younger. You should get your eyes tested every year at your age, and I don't want to be spending all my time visiting you in hospital.'

'Someone knocked into me, not the other way around!' It didn't seem to matter; she was still under the misconception that I was at least partially to blame.

I did, however phone Jules up later, telling her exactly what had happened and admitting that I might have let my stupidity blow all chances of getting into Goodfellow's gym.

'Don't worry yourself over that, we'll just have to find a Plan B,' she said.

I just grunted. What more could I do?

Jules was very interested in the details of the car park incident, and I used WhatsApp to send over to her copies of the photographs and the short video I had taken of Barry Spencer and myself immediately following our little ruckus. I felt it best to have a few other people fully aware, just in case there came a follow-on incident at some time.

'Have you told Sal? What did she have to say?'

'I gave her an overview, but I didn't want to worry her unnecessarily. I wasn't hurt, and she would be upset.'

'You're treading on dangerous ground there, Chilli. It might not have been a lie, but it was pretty close to being one. And if I were her, I would be definitely telling you that you had broken 'Rule 6' of what we had all agreed to. You ever try downplaying an incident like that to me and believe me, you will end up regretting it.'

She was right, and I knew it, but this was our first assignment, and I didn't want it to fall apart just because I had foolishly opened my big mouth at the wrong time when sulking because I couldn't get in to see Goodfellow's gym the day before.

I mulled things over in my mind for the rest of the day, thinking of what my next move might be. One thing was sure; I had to learn as much as I possibly could about this bloke Gary Goodfellow and his pet ape Barry Spencer.

It was later in the afternoon when I 'Messaged' my pal Pete Tanger to ask when a good time for a brief chat about my search for Sam White might be. It took Pete a couple of hours to come back to me. I figured he was probably out on the golf course when my message went through, and I was right.

He phoned me back around 5 p.m.

'Whatcha Chilli. You after me?'

'Yes, hope I didn't get in the way of your golf.'

'Nothing gets in the way of my golf. What can I do for you?'

'Pete, what can you tell me about a guy called Gary Goodfellow and his pet ape, Barry Spencer?'

'That pair?' He hesitated for a brief second, then, 'I was wondering if they might have some involvement in this. You know Gary Goodfellow, he is Tim Goodfellow's son. The prop who used to play in the second team up at the club back in the nineties. He died some years back from a heart attack, but his son has played for the club for a number of years. I hear on the grapevine that the Club Committee are looking at throwing him out and banning him from the Club. They should have done that years ago; the guy is bad news.'

'Why would they throw him out?' I asked.

'Word is he is into selling drugs - he has been acting unofficially as an assistant coach with Colt's team, but I reckon that is just an avenue for getting 'an in' with the younger players for his drug sales. Apart from that, there has been some talk of him generally being a bloody nuisance with the ladies - the girlfriends and wives of some of the lads. In the end, the Committee is going to terminate his membership, but this is all unofficial at the moment. When they finally get their act into order, Goodfellow will be told he is unwelcome in the Club anymore. Bloody good job, too. It should have happened years ago.

He is not a nice bloke at all, he tries to build up a gangster image of himself with people he meets for the first time, but ninety percent of it is all bullshit. I think I told you about him before. Call himself 'The Tooth Fairy' and claimed he would use a pair of pliers to pull the teeth out of anyone who crossed him. All bullshit, though. Never met anyone who lost a tooth to him.'

'What about his mate Barry Spencer?'

'Another twat. 'Blow Torch', I ask you? These silly gangster names they make up for themselves to sound tough. Bloody idiots. The pair of them were dealing with drugs, and probably still are, a couple of nasty little clowns you don't want to associate with. 'Blow Torch' and 'The Tooth Fairy', I ask you? The lads used to call them 'Blow-wave' and the 'Poof Fairy.' He laughed his way through the last sentence.

'Some sort of second vision there, then,' I said. ''Poof Fairy' was the name I called him the other day, as well.'

'Great minds think alike, but there again, you never were one to come up with anything original. But watch them, Chil; they are a couple of nasty, spiteful little gits. Best to avoid them if you can.'

'When you say Goodfellow was annoying some of the player's wives and girlfriends, what exactly was it he was doing?'

'Well, it was never clearly spelt out, but the word was he was trying-it-on with the women. No one in particular, just anyone he could impress with his smooth talk. Buying them drinks when their boyfriends or husbands were still in the showers - after the game - right twat. Not choosy at all, anything in a skirt was a target. A couple of the lads got quite pissed off about it. Never amounted to anything you could actually lay at his door. Just a slimeball, looking for his chances.'

'Are these clowns likely to be a serious physical threat to me? Or any of my team? Do I have anything to be worried about?'

'Well, I wouldn't turn my back on either of them and watch yourself if you ever go down a dark alley near where they live, but apart from that, you're best just keeping out of their way.'

'Too late for that, I'm afraid. I had a run-in with Goodfellow's pet monkey this morning and have just dropped him off at the A&E.'

'You're joking?'

'Nope, hit him with a chair leg. (I know that, actually, that wasn't strictly true and that it was a stool leg I had hit him with, but chair leg is what came out in the telling).

'Bloody Hell, good on ya. I'm sure the twat deserved it.'

'He did.'

'Watch your back Chilli. Those toe-rags aren't the sort you want to associate with. Call on me if you need any help. I'm sure some of the old guys will turn up if you need back-up at any time.'

'Oh yeah, a vigilante gang of sixty and seventy-year-olds striking fear into the criminal classes.'

I heard Pete laugh down the other end of the phone, then. 'Got to go, mate, need a pee.'

'Common problem at our age. Hey?'

I laughed but appreciated the offer of help. Not that I needed it yet; after all, I was the guy in his mid-seventies who had just dropped a dozy thug off at the A&E. Still got a few tricks up my sleeve - thinking of my stool leg. 'There's life in the old dog yet', I thought, beginning to feel a bit better about myself, a silly self-satisfied smirk on my face.

O-O-O

The next day, at around 10 in the morning, I got a phone call out of the blue from Goodfellow himself.

'Hi Chilli Pepper? Sorry I missed you the other day, I was doing a bit of 'one-on-one' personal training for a client on a pre-booked appointment basis. I have to close up the gym when that happens.'

'Okay, I can go along with that.' I said, but it seemed a bit strange. Not a sensible way to run a business. Still, what do I know about running a business? I'm still new to the game.

'So, you are thinking of joining one of my personal fitness programmes, I gather? Would you just be looking at an open gym membership or a more personalised programme?'

I couldn't believe it. I had thought I had blown my chances of getting in to see inside his gym, and here he was, offering me an invite to visit. 'Don't blow this.' I thought, 'Just go with the flow.'

'Can't say, I'm not really decided yet. What sort of thing do you offer with the personalised programmes?' I said.

'That depends on what you are looking to achieve. Is your prime goal to get fitter, or is it to lose weight? I call it fitness or fatness. What is it you are looking for?'

'Well, I'm not sure, I just think I should be doing something - not too strenuous at my age, but something to keep me trim and healthy. I'd like to take a look at what you have. See if there's something that might work for me - at the right price, of course!'

'Of course, there's bound to be one of our programmes that you will be interested in. If not, we can always put together a personalised plan specifically designed to meet your needs.'

Very strange, I thought, no mention at all of his buddy Barry Spencer and our little scuffle the other day. It was as if the car park incident had never happened. Did this guy think I hadn't connected what had happened in the car park with him? Or was he trying to disassociate himself from Spencer's failed attempt to scare me off?

'So, are you inviting me over to take a look at your gym and see what, if anything, you can offer me in a personal training package then?'

It looked like I might getting my chance to see inside his health centre after all!

'Yeah, come on over early tomorrow evening, say around 5 pm? I can take you through a programme I think should work well for you. Maybe we could go for a pint after if you don't have to rush back?'

'Can we make it Tuesday? I've got a few things I need to sort out tomorrow. Oh, and can I assume gym membership, if I sign up, might come with 'mate's rates'?'

'Of course, I can always sort out something special for my rugger buddies. Especially when they were pals of my old man, you come on over and let's talk things through. Bring your kit. You can get a shower over here.'

Right, I thought, that hadn't gone the way I imagined. I've got an unexpected invitation to visit his gym, something I hadn't been expecting. All very strange, had I missed something? I couldn't believe that he seemed to think I was that gullible. He had to have realised my connection to Haley White through the silly throwaway jibe he got from me when I tried to call in at his gym yesterday. He had sent his 'pet ape' Blower over to try to put the frighteners on me and now was pretending that it hadn't happened. Ridiculous, what

226

planet do these morons come from? All I could do was play along and see where this path would take me.

'Okay, I'm game for that. 5 pm, you say? See you then. Oh, and how is Blowjob?' I thought I would throw another brick in the pond to see what reaction it might trigger.

'Blowjob?'

'Yes, I think that's what they call him. The bald-headed guy who works for you?'

'Oh, Barry? I haven't seen him much at all this week, I think he has been down in London with his brother. If I see him, I'll tell him you've been asking after him. Didn't know you knew him.'

'We crossed paths briefly sometime back; forget it, I doubt he will remember me.'

If he doesn't remember me, I thought, that will probably be down to his concussion. This couldn't be right, there is no way I could be so lucky.

All very strange - either this guy is 'a penny short of a pound' or I am, I thought. Does he really think I'm falling for that crap? Or maybe he just doesn't care?

I needed to talk with 'the Sap-laf-fea crew'. There would, no doubt, be concerns raised and offers to accompany me, but I didn't think it would work if we all turned up over there. I had somehow to get my hands on his phone and, I assume, his Pin, or password, or whatever's needed to access his picture files. It started to sound a bit like 'Mission Impossible' when I boiled it down like that. Maybe there was another way of getting into this somehow? Mal would know.

What about Goodfellow's pal Barry? I wondered, is there some way I might isolate him and then tighten the screws there somehow to get him to come over onto our side? A possibility? There was the distinct possibility that he might have had a run-in with the law at some time in the past. Was it worth doing a bit more digging on that side of things - maybe something Mal or Jules could look into?

Barry was Goodfellow's gofer, but I knew nothing about what sort of a person he was when not under the influence of his master. Did he have any principles at all? Or was he just the moron he gave the impression of being?

Pete Tanger was also someone I should tap up for information on that side of things, he might have an opening into Barry. I made a mental note to ask Pete to do a little more digging for me on that. This will cost me a pint, I had no doubt.

Chapter 21 - On the Right Track

Monday 6th/2

Monday morning on the 6th of February was a bitterly cold one, but at least it was dry. There had been an overnight frost, and even as late as ten in the morning, it still clung onto those areas not directly in the path of the rising sun.

Last night, before going to bed, I had told Sally of Goodfellow's invitation for me to visit his gym on Tuesday, which was the following day.

It was like I had opened a beehive. Any thoughts I might have harboured of driving over to Goodfellow's gym on my own went out of the window. Sally made it clear that my visiting the gym was putting me needlessly in danger, and I was not to even think of going there on my own.

'You don't have a frigging clue as to what you might be walking into. Sometimes I think you need a sodding nursemaid! You're a walking catastrophe waiting to happen!'

She reinforced her insistence by telephoning Jules to let her know where she stood on the matter.

Jules took 'no prisoners' with her anger at me.

'Put him on the phone, Sal. I need to speak to him.' I could hear her voice shout down the phone in Jules' hand.

Jules thrust her phone at me, and then the diatribe started.

'Who the hell gave you the 'God-Given right' to take over all the action roles in this business? Who the bloody hell do you think you are? Jack bloody Reacher? We are supposed to be a team. Solve problems with our research and intelligence, and there you are, fighting with bloody morons in car parks and walking into obvious danger without backup. There is no 'I' in team,' you know. We all agreed to stick with a set of bloody rules, which you were instrumental in creating. If you don't start playing by the same rules as the rest of us, then I'm out of this business, and I mean it!'

Wow, that sat me back. Sure, I felt there might be some concern about me going into Goodfellow's gym on my own, but I didn't think that accepting the invitation was going to stir up quite such a shitstorm.

'We agreed, as a team, that any significant course of action would only take place if all the team members were in agreement. We agreed the course of action would be tailored to the best 'agents' suited for the task, and there would be no 'Knights in armour' riding into the dragon's den on their own. What makes you think you are the best one to visit the gym? What is it you think you will be able to do there on your own? Given his approach to anything in a skirt, why shouldn't I be the one to visit him in his gym? Is it because I'm a woman? Is it because you think I'm not 'man' enough?'

'No, I just, I just, erm…...'

'You just thought there could be some danger here - so the poor little women must stay at home and keep safe.'

That was a bit unfair, I thought. I hadn't had time to think through anything of the sort. But I could see that this was not going to be an argument I had any chance of winning.

'What is it you think you could hope to achieve from a visit to Goodfellow's gym?' Jules asked.

'Well, I thought I might be able to see first-hand what type of mobile phone he has and maybe if he has a computer or iPad,' I was struggling here for something to say, 'or - I don't know - something.'

'And you are the best person to recognise these computer - camera devices and opportunities, are you?'

A long couple of seconds went by as if she was expecting me to answer then, 'No - no - you're not, are you? Nor am I, but we do have someone in the team who has the skills and expertise to recognise all those sorts of things.'

She, of course, meant Mal, and she was right. Not only that but taking a male friend along to also see the facilities in the gym should not - in normal circumstances - raise any concerns with Goodfellow. I could always say that I had mentioned that I was thinking of joining a gym to my friend Mal, and he thought that it was something he might like to do, also. Maybe we could both do it, join, I mean, together?

I also had to accept that Goodfellow was well-aware that I was in some way connected to Haley White after I had stupidly blurted it out the other day, and I couldn't see how it was plausible that he might have missed the fact that I had put his pal Barry Spencer in hospital.

'Do you think Mal will be okay to come over with me?' I asked Jules.

'Well, if he is not, you will have to make other arrangements for your visit find a time when Mal can be there.' That was that.

I had to admit to myself that, with Mal along and his skills with regard to mobile phones and computers, it was starting to feel like there was now a purposeful shape to the visit to Goodfellow's gym, rather than just the 'go-look-see' I had been planning. It was almost beginning to look as though there was some semblance to it being a 'planned event' with a purpose rather than the rag-tag adventure I had initially intended.

'I'll talk to Mal,' Jules said, 'To make sure he is free to come over with you, and we will all agree beforehand as to what the purpose of the visit is. What is the name of the gym?

Where is it? And what time are you supposed to meet with Goodfellow?'

I gave Jules the details.

'Assuming he is free to come, I suggest you pick up Mal from his house on the way over to Goodfellow's. It's on your way, and it will give you both time to get your stories aligned. It will also give you the chance to make sure Mal knows everything beforehand. No holding anything back.'

Half an hour later, Jules rang to say Mal was free all day tomorrow and Wednesday if we needed him.

'I've given him the low-down on what has happened so far, he is pretty much up to speed - unless there are any other little secrets you still haven't shared with us.'

She had to get that last jibe in.

'I suggested he might want to 'brush up' on what and where you can store videos and how you can erase them - if possible, remotely. He was pretty sure he could manage to do something to trash Goodfellow's video files. Apparently any difficulty on that side depended on what sort of systems Goodfellow had used when storing them. Mal doesn't seem to think access to Passwords and PIN codes and all that shit will be too much of a hindrance. I said if he could access Goodfellow's files, it might be interesting to see what other stuff he might have stored away. Told him to just see what

233

you can find. He's on board, I said you would pick him up at 3 pm tomorrow afternoon.'

'Three? We don't need to be there until 5 pm, and it's only a twenty-minute drive.'

'You can take him for a coffee and a bacon sandwich first on your way there. Use the time to get to know him a bit better and bring him fully up to speed on everything, and I mean every-bloody-thing that has been going on. Rule bloody 6, remember. If you hold anything back on this, you will need to look for a new partner, and I mean it.'

'Okay, I'm sorry, I'm still kinda new at all of this. I thought I was doing the right thing, but I was wrong and I know now. You're right. I'm sure I will make mistakes in the future, but I promise to learn from them and never purposefully hold any information back from the team.'

'We don't need to take this any further until you 'cock up' again next time. I accept you were doing what you thought was the right thing, but we are a team, and it is bloody essential we work as a team. Mal is an important part of this team, and I want you to recognise it and him to feel it.'

'Is he a brown sauce or a tomato sauce man?'

'What the hell are you talking about?'

'Mal I mean. I just wanted to know if he was the sort of guy who liked brown sauce, or tomato sauce, on his bacon sandwich.'

'Piss off, you daft sod.' Jules ended the call, but not before I caught the smile in her voice.

I hadn't poisoned the water of our friendship too much, and I was beginning to feel there was hope that we would soon be starting to get back onto good terms again. I had taken my warning from both Jules and Sal seriously - the message had struck home.

That evening, Sal and I had talked the matter through, and I felt we had also reached an acceptable agreement with me promising to always keep her fully up to speed on what assignments the Sap-laf-fea team were working on.

She, in turn, agreed not to hit me too hard with any heavy implements if I ever forgot my promise.

Chapter 22 - Back to School

Tuesday 7th/2 am

The next morning was a Tuesday - Sal, in her smart office clothing, offset a little by the Doc Martens 1460 black lace-up boots I had bought her for her birthday, had driven off early for work at around eight-thirty. At least it was early for her, not for me. I was up and breakfasted before she left, fed the two cats, medicated the older one with his Meloxicam drops, and took Truffle out for her early morning 'walkies'. The normal sequence of my morning activities.

Sal and I had pecked a kiss with one another before she left, which indicated to me that I was back in the good books if not fully forgiven.

I hadn't slept that well that night. There was too much going on in my mind; different approaches I might take, difficulties we might need to find a way around, and the remnants of guilt lingering from the 'telling off' I had received the previous day. We were in a difficult situation with no simple answers; there were still too many things we just didn't know. One of those predicaments was that, without crossing over and coming up with a solution which might lie outside of the law, it would be difficult to find a clear path through the maze needed to achieve a satisfactory outcome for Haley. I also had to accept that I was still on probation and had a few 'bridges to mend' with people, those I needed to convince that I really was a team player. I had said all the right words, but - as the idiom goes - 'actions speak louder than words'.

I had dressed with some forethought in jeans, a short-sleeved tee shirt, and a loose black microfleece top. It may not sound too impressive, but there was 'method in my madness', and had given careful thought in what I chose to wear for my meeting with Goodfellow.

It was another frosty morning, and - trying to win back a few 'brownie points' - I had even offered Sally the use of my Evoque to drive to work because of the icy back roads leading out of the village.

She hesitated for a brief second, seemingly giving it some consideration before telling me, 'No, I'll stick with my own car, thanks. It's too much trouble to swap all my 'nik naks' over. I always drive extra carefully around the back road past the Crematorium, and once I get onto the main roads, they tend to be sanded when the weather is like this. Anyway, you've got to pick up Mal. You're better going over to Mal's in the Evoque.'

That suited me, Sal's small Ford was fine, but you get used to your own car, and I was comfortable with my Evoque, now I had managed to find my way around the dashboard instrumentation, and the heated seats and steering wheel were a godsend in this sort of weather. Anyway, the offer had been genuine, which was the main thing, and it meant I didn't need to surreptitiously slip the leadwood stool leg out of my car and over into hers without it being spotted.

I still had a bit of time before I was scheduled to collect Mal and take him for a bacon sandwich and given the direction this assignment seemed to be heading, I thought I could best use the time trying to nurture some sort of understanding about how stored information on mobile phone and computers worked. It was Mal's area of expertise I knew, and I wasn't trying to become an expert, I just didn't want to appear a complete numpty when it came to talking with him about the basics of cyber security.

I keyed into Google on my iPad and began a search into Cyber Security, Trojan Horse programmes, Worms, and malware, taking in just enough of the basics to understand what some of the terminology meant.

I started with Cyber Security, after all, that was Mal's area of expertise, and I had to accept it was remiss of me not to have looked into it earlier, at some point before he had joined the team. In fairness, I guess I had just assumed that, because it was something to do with computers and while it might be useful to know, it would also be highly technical geek stuff, which no doubt would involve terminology that would definitely challenge my understanding.

Simplistically (and it has to be simplistic for my basic understanding), cybersecurity is how people and businesses protect the information stored on their smartphones, computers, and the internet. How they restrict and protect access to their online banking, emails, and anything else we store online nowadays, from cyber criminals seeking to gain access to it. There you go, it was basic, but a one-sentence explanation I understood and I was pretty pleased with that.

I learnt that Trojan horse malware, tricks its way into a computer, and presumably a mobile phone, by pretending to be bona fide software. Once inside, 'attackers' are then able to take control of the computer, upload or download files, and change or delete information as if they were the legitimate user. Trojans are not likely to spread automatically. They usually stay at the infected host only.

A 'computer worm', however, goes one step further than the Trojan malware in that it can propagate, or self-replicate, from one computer to another without human activation once the transgressor has managed to breach a system. Typically, a worm spreads across a network through the Internet or LAN (Local Area Network) connection.

That was enough, I was happy to settle with that. It was a useful bit of background research, the sort of thing real

Private Enquiry Agents do. It gave me a modicum of hope that, if we could somehow breach the safeguards on Goodfellow's smartphone or computer, Mal might be able to clean out the recording related to Haley's rape. Failing that, maybe find some other sort of leverage we could use, to stop Goodfellow in his tracks.

I was feeling a little more comfortable with my newly gained knowledge about cyber malware. Don't get me wrong, I do not feel embarrassed that nearly everyone I know, including my wife and kids - are far more capable when it comes to using computers and the Apps on their smartphones. But it's not comfortable to be the only one in the room in the dark when everyone else seems to be talking a different language. At least now, I wouldn't feel quite so lost and could appear to be understanding any conversations where malware was the subject being discussed.

With that basic knowledge in mind, I set off to find Mal's house in Keresley. I didn't think it would be too difficult to find; after all, it was close to Corby, and I had driven that way nearly every week during the playing season in my rugby playing days. To be on the safe side, I entered Mal's address into the satnav in my car before I set off.

One other task, just prior to leaving home, was to do a check on the 'Private Enquiry Agent field kit' that I had put together for just such an occasion. Pencil and pink notebook, reading glasses, my little can of red dye spray, which fitted in the pocket of the gilet that I intended to wear over my fleece jumper, a 'personal alarm device' now attached to my car key ring, mobile phone, wallet, and broken stool leg. Raring to go.

The broken stool leg was now safely stored in the driver's side door pocket of my car. I had needed to move an ice scraper and a few other things out to make room for it, but there it sat, ready for use for the time being. I hadn't planned on using some of these items, but I felt it was good practice to adopt and check that they were all there and ready if needed, and I planned on taking the stool leg with me for reassurance when I visited Goodfellow's gym.

Stool leg aside, I would run a check with Mal to ensure that he was also equipped and ready for our meeting with Goodfellow - I guess he would also have a few things of his own - some other sort of additional kit, more specific to his line of expertise.

The traffic was light by the time I set off, at around 2:15, which is understandable for the time of day as most people would be at work, school, or working from home, the latter being more prevalent since the recent pandemic. So what little traffic there was on the A46 were mainly lorries and delivery trucks interspersed with just the odd car here and there. The outside temperature had begun to warm up a little since Sally had set off for college this morning. Still a bright day, not a cloud in the sky.

No need to rush, I stopped off at the Shell petrol station and topped the car fuel tank up with diesel. I guess I was feeling somewhat apprehensive about our appointment to meet Gary Goodfellow. Understandable, I suppose, I still wasn't sure what to expect. It didn't feel like I was fully in control of the game, that uneasy feeling, more like I was being carried along by events rather than them being of my own making.

On the plus side of things, however, I did have Mal with me, which Goodfellow wouldn't be expecting. I also had something in the shape of an idea of what we might be able to do to remove the threat to Haley's reputation, not to mention the relationship with her family.

I pulled up outside Mal's house about 20 minutes later. Starting to feel a bit of a headache coming on - too much thinking and worry, probably.

Mal's place was a neat mid-terrace brick building somewhat similar in looks to my old house in Rothesay Avenue, so it was probably built around the late 1940's. The front of the building was pebble-dashed, which took in the whole of the first floor above the ground floor windows at the front of the building. White painted window frames, with black exterior windowsills and a black front door, like nearly every other house in the street, but Mal's paintwork looked pristine like it had recently been redecorated. Externally, only the numbers on the doors denoted the difference from one house to the next.

Mal's house had a small, neatly trimmed front lawn, with the obligatory, also neatly trimmed, six-foot-high privet hedge providing a degree of privacy from the eyes of anyone walking past. Again, the garden reflected my impression of the man - neatly trimmed and very private. Even here in the middle of winter, everything was as it should be, not a weed evident in the flowerbeds edging the lawn. All of the dead flower heads and dead leaves had been removed, and it looked like everything was ready, just waiting patiently for when the spring flowers would emerge.

Four large terracotta plant pots lined the short, paved path, two on either side, leading up to the front door. The pots were empty but cleaned and ready for whatever would be planted in them the coming Spring.

Just as I was about to open Mal's gate, a magpie took flight from his lawn - 'One for sorrow,' I thought, my right hand coming up to my forehead in a salute and a whistle just beginning to form and emit from my mouth. I stopped in my tracks, halting my entrance just in time to see a second magpie taking flight to follow its mate. Two for joy. I wouldn't have called myself superstitious, but my nervous self felt it would welcome any bit of luck passing my way, even that arising from an old superstition.

I pressed the doorbell and could hear a chiming from inside the house, notifying the occupant of my arrival, and after a short wait, no more than a few seconds, Mal was there to invite me in.

'Yo Chilli, how's it going?' A bright, friendly greeting and a welcoming smile lit up his face. His aftershave hit me full on, I caught my breath before speaking.

'Hi Mal, not too early, am I?'

'No, no, spot on. Go on in.'

Mal let me lead the way from his hallway straight on through into the kitchen area, patting me on the shoulder in greeting.

There he was again, I thought, looking like a male model, someone who had just stepped out of a 'Joe Browns' magazine. Suede Hush Puppies type shoes, blue jeans with turn-ups, a red and blue paisley shirt, topped with a biscuit-coloured waistcoat.

I had to think he had dressed up specially for me and for the trip out to see Goodfellow - no one wears this sort of designer gear for sitting around the house. I trusted the liberal application of aftershave wasn't something he was wearing just for me.

'Would you like a cup of tea before we go?' He graciously asked.

'Well, Jules suggested we should go out for a coffee and a bacon sandwich on our way to meet the Tooth Fairy. Give me a chance to bring you fully up to speed with things as I know them. Is that okay?'

Did I imagine it, or did his eyes really light up at the mention of Jules' name?

'Yes, well, we can't argue with the 'little madam', can we? I know a nice little cafe on the way over to Bedworth - Molly's. I used to use it a lot when I was still in the Police. Be good to take a look in, see what the old girl's up to and what's changed over the last few years.'

'How close is it to Goodfellow's gym?' I asked.

'If the gym is where I think it is, it is just around the corner. About half a mile or so at the outside.'

'Great.' I said, 'Let's go. I must admit I haven't had much of a breakfast, and a bacon sandwich would go down well now.'

'Just got to feed the cat first, if you can spare a minute.'

Mal took out a sachet of cat food from his cupboard by the sink and emptied half of it into a saucer-sized metal cat dish. The sound of the dish being rattled worked like a doorbell, and out of nowhere, there appeared a beautiful, sleek white and black Siamese cat. It didn't even deign to look in my direction, it just slinked up to its food dish and delicately began to eat.

For some reason, the thought went through my mind; if Mal was to have a cat, this would be the one he would choose, and if this cat were to choose someone to be its owner, it would be Mal. They were made for one another.

'Beautiful cat.'

'Freya, quite a character. I think she thinks she owns me.'

Mal bent down to fondle Freya's ears as she ate, then stood and grabbed a navy blue blazer, which had been hanging, from a coat hanger hooked onto the back of one of his kitchen chairs. It fitted in with the rest of his clothes well, as I might have guessed it would. I'm certainly no fashion buff, but even I accepted the guy has taste.

'Should I take my car?'

'No, hop in mine, more time to chat. Have you got all the things you might need?'

'Spectacles, Testicles, Wallet and Watch. You mean?'

'Yeah, and any computer thingy-ma-jigs.'

'I've got a couple of things, but I can't be sure what I might need until I see what the size of the challenge might be. I'll stick in a couple of extra things and leave them in your car if that's okay with you, my MacBook Pro and a few gizmo widgets - will that be okay?'

This, I sensed, was a bit of a test for me to see just how computer-illiterate I really was. I knew what a MacBook Pro was. I had a MacBook Air of my own and chose, when buying it a few years back, to look into whether it was sensible for me to pay the extra and go for the Pro version at the time. Fiscal sense prevailed and gave me the sensible answer. For the sort of use I would be putting it to, I went for the cheaper of the two options. But widgets? By chance, I knew there were some sort of computer programmes that are similar to Apps. What they did and how they worked, I had no idea, but I knew that Mal would not be loading them into the back of my car.

'How many widgets have you got?' I asked. 'Will I need to drop the back seats down?'

Mal smiled - he realised I had seen through his little ploy.

'Only joking,' he said. 'Just wanted to get some understanding of just how computer savvy you were. Didn't get much of a handle on it from when we were playing the 'Search Game' a few weeks back.'

'No worry, best treating me like I know nothing. Just keep in mind that I am pretty well at a loss when it comes down to most things that wander outside the basics of Google Mail, WhatsApp, and Office. Oh, I do know that you can only access WhatsApp through your phone, not your iPad.' I felt quite pleased with myself at this.

Mal told me that restricted access to WhatsApp through iPad would be likely to change soon.

He smiled and held out his hand. 'Sorry about that. I wasn't trying to trick you, I just wanted to know what level of detail I might need to go into when explaining what we were dealing with.'

I shook his hand, 'No worry - if you do need to explain anything to me, you would be best assuming my knowledge of computers and cyber security is lower Primary School.'

'Actually, kids in Primary Schools are generally quite switched on these days.' He gave a bit of a pained smile. 'I need a couple of Aspirin before we go, I can feel the beginnings of a migraine coming on. Need to nip it in the bud.'

I waited as he popped in a couple of white pills and took a sip of water. Then he smiled over at me.

'That should do the job. Are you ready to roll?'

'You bet. Bacon sandwich - look out - here I come.'

Mal loaded his computer bag, a rather 'cool' distressed canvas backpack - this guy truly was quite at the peak of fashion - into the back of my car, checked the back door of his house was locked, grabbed his phone and front door keys, and off we went.

Before we reached the end of his road, Mal had looked up and found the name of the cafe we were heading for on his phone and read me the postcode, which, as I was already driving, he entered into my Satnav for me. That done, we headed off on the designated route.

Mal actually knew the way to the cafe without the need of my Satnav and could have directed us verbally, but I still preferred having it programmed in, it gave me an overview of the immediate surrounding area and the reassurance that I had some control of the journey.

Traffic was still light, and we arrived at the cafe - Molly's Eating House - in less than an hour. I found a free parking space just on the opposite side of the road to Molly's place and tucked my car into it.

The cafe wasn't very big at all, probably a converted shop, I thought, just enough room in the front area for the till counter and six small plywood and tin tables - the type that can easily be folded away when the need arises. As dining areas go, despite Mal's recommendations, it didn't look that amazing, but the smell of the cooking bacon filled the room and wafted out through the front door like a lure to attract any passers-by.

There were no other customers in the cafe at the time, so we had our choice of where to sit. We picked a table towards the back of the cafe, away from the front window. Mal had brought his MacBook Pro with him. I didn't think he'd need it yet, but I didn't say anything. I brought my pink notebook.

'This place should be in the Michelin Guide.' Mal told me. 'The bacon and egg sandwiches are the best in the Midlands.'

'Are you a brown sauce or a tomato sauce person?' I asked.

He looked at me, a little frown showing as he re-ran what I had just asked him through his mind.

'Brown sauce, of course. I'm not a Southerner.'

'That's great, I'll get these. What is it you want?' I asked as a short, round elderly lady who looked as if she had quite often partaken of the cakes and bacon sandwiches herself, over the years, came over to take our order.

This, I assumed, was Molly, as she, being the only one there, appeared to be both the waitress and bacon chef as well.

'Hello, my luvies, what can I get you? Got some real nice pork sausages. My husband is the butcher, and he tells me that these are some of the tastiest he has ever made.'

I shared a look with Mal. We had both entered the cafe with bacon sandwiches in mind, but after this pitch on the sausages, my mind was in turmoil.

I broke the momentary silence, 'Can I have a bacon and egg sandwich toasted and perhaps a couple of your sausages as well?'

'Course you can luvie.' She scribbled something down with her pencil onto the pad of paper she was holding.

'Sounds like a good choice.' Mal piped in. 'I'll go with the same. Do you have any black pudding? No, no - forget that - too much - just the bacon and egg sandwich and the sausages, please.'

'Are you sure? Yes? Right. And will you be wanting cups of tea?'

We both ordered cups of tea, and the waitress/chef/owner disappeared off into her kitchen.

'You could have had some black pudding if you wanted it, you know. I wouldn't have minded stretching the expenses to cover it?'

'No, you're okay, Julie told me you'd sulk if I went wild with my food allowance.'

The cafe was nice and warm, and I slipped off my parka, letting it fall back over my chair. Mal took off his scarf, neatly folding it and placing it alongside his calfskin gloves on the empty table next to ours.

Sitting back in my chair, I stretched out my legs, taking care not to kick Mal as I got into a comfortable position.

'Chilli, there's something I was wanting to ask you.'

'Yes?'

'Your relationship with Julie?'

'Yes?'

'Well, I mean. Are you cousins or something?'

'What makes you say that?'

'Well, it's difficult to put my thumb on it; I haven't known you that long. It's just that I notice some of your mannerisms, the way you act, your way of thinking. I don't know. It just seems very much aligned with Julie's. Like you're both related somehow.'

I gave what I guess I thought was a whimsical smile. There it was again, only this time taking the supposition that the relationship between our parents dated perhaps further back in time than Jules and I had previously surmised and that she and I might possibly be closer than we, or at least I, cared to think.

'No - no - no.' I stammered but maintained my smile as I said it.

'It's just one of those things. A coincidence, I guess. Don't worry about it, though. Sal seems to see the same sort of similarities. Just one of those things.'

'I've known her for over ten years and thought she was one of a kind, then you come along, and it feels like there's two of her.'

'We've known each other since we were kids, nothing more than that. Let's just leave it there.' I gave him a big, friendly smile to assure him that I wasn't offended at all.

'So, let's talk about how we are going to handle this business with Goodfellow.' I said, bringing the reason for us being there to the front.

'Well, I think we both agree that our primary goal is to see what we can do to remove and destroy the video Goodfellow has of Haley. Yes?'

'You've got it.'

'Right', he said. 'There are a couple of approaches we can take; one, we can try to convince him that he needs to surrender it to us or face legal consequences. Or, as we had discussed when we were talking with Sally and Julie, I can get into his computer files and erase the video without his permission. I think we both know that it is the second option that is the most likely to be the safest.'

'What would you need to do that?'

'What do you know about malware?' he asked.

I told him I had the basics, Worms, and Trojans, and that was about it. I could see that I surprised him, he hadn't thought I would have had any knowledge on the subject.

'I'm impressed,' he said. 'With most people over the age of fifty, it's all computer dark arts and black magic. Mysterious things that happen in the 'iClouds' and think that Personal Hotspots are things you get in your pants after an especially hot curry. Best you leave it at that, I can give you an hour or so on Cyber Security another day, when we have some spare time. I can explain it in simple terms as an overview, but for this case, all you need to know is that I have to get my hands on his mobile phone for, ideally, an hour at the outside, but probably just five minutes will do. I can download whatever's there onto my phone, all of the trash he has on file, and replace it, in his files, with cartoons.'

'I get the downloading and removing of the files, but why replace it with cartoons?'

'Well, it depends on what mobile device he has, whether it's an iPhone, an iPad, or an Android. The principle is the same for all in general; you get into the files and delete them. However, it's not always that simple. If it's an Android, although you have deleted the file, the Android does not actually remove it from the storage drive. It just hides it so you think it's deleted by marking that space in the file as being empty, but in actuality, the file is physically still there, so it can be recovered by someone who knows what they are doing. It's how Government Agencies are able to pull data off wiped hard drives. I've had to do a lot of that in my time with Cyber Security.'

'So what you are saying is that they are there forever?'

'No, nothing so dramatic. The files are still there, but only until you manage to save another file on top in that same spot - it doesn't have to be cartoons; any sort of data rubbish will do. Simply put, we could wipe the files off whatever device Goodfellow has them stored on, but he could still go to someone with the know-how who would be able, using an 'Undeleter' app, to recover them. And there are plenty of spotty, snotty teenage nerds around who would do it for the drugs or money.'

'There has to be some way of cleaning out the files, surely?'

'Yes, of course. There is a wonderful app - that I just happen to have access to - which, once we have got into his storage drive, will overwrite the empty space in the drive with random bits of data, then delete the end product. Jess has helped me fine-tune it a bit made it pretty simple and quick to activate now A big smile on his face. 'It's kinda magic,' he sang at me, his smile turning into something of a cheesy grin. 'You really are lucky to have me on your team.'

'Humph!' I grunted. He was starting to sound like me.

'Any files previously deleted will then be permanently erased, making it virtually impossible for anyone, even the nerds, being able to recover them.'

'Nothing to it then?' I said, 'And it's our team, not my team.'

'Right, Boss,' he smiled. 'Do you know, I reckon I played against Goodfellow's dad back in the old days. A prop, wasn't he? Dirty player!'

'Yes, not a nice guy, I had a run-in with him myself, off the pitch, back in the days.'

'Sounds like the bad genes have passed through onto his son.'

I couldn't argue with that.

'What else do we need to know before we go in there?' Mal asked.

'I dun-know. We will have to play a lot of this by ear. Maybe we get nowhere, maybe we spot something we might be able to use. If the chance arises where you can get a hold of his mobile for a short spell, use it. Get your 'worm', or whatever, implanted, and we can beat a hasty retreat.'

We chatted a while longer, nursing our teas and, as I had promised to Jules, I made sure Mal was fully up to speed with everything that had happened, including my run-in with

Barry 'The Blowtorch' Spencer in Sainsbury's car park, and his subsequent need to visit the A&E in Warwick.

That bit of my carpark experience, I noticed, brought a smile to Mal's face.

'I wish I could have seen that.' He hesitated for a second or so, then, 'You are going to have to take care with this Chilli; these people are not the sort to just let grievances like this go. We need to get something, if we can, that we can hold over them to stop any retaliation at some later stage when we least expect it.'

I could see the sense of what Mal was implying. Something to think about and add to my worries when I found time to look beyond the present.

Time had moved on at quite a pace since we first sat down in Molly's, and it was already starting to get that early evening darkness outside.

Chapter 23 - The Tooth Fairy's Lair

Tuesday 7th/2, early evening

'You ready to roll?' I asked.

'Let's go.' He said, and we both stood and began wrapping ourselves up in coats and scarves before setting off on the next step of our journey.

'Do you need to go to the toilet before we go?' He added.

'Don't you start.'

I left a healthy tip for Molly; the food had been good, and she had left us alone for well over an hour without any interruptions or obvious signs of listening in to our conversations.

'You take care, luvvies, come back soon.' She called to us as we left.

We both waved and made our way back across the road to my car.

When we were both seated and strapped in the Evoque, I pulled the stool leg out of my side door pocket and pushed it up the left sleeve of my fleece so that it rested against my lower arm just above my wrist, the elasticated band at the bottom of my fleece sleeve effectively stopping it from falling out unintentionally.

'You're expecting trouble, I see.' Mel noted.

'Just covering my bets. Have you got anything? Your dye spray?'

'Just my suave nature and good looks.' he said, 'Oh, and.' He tapped the area over his heart. I thought it was going to be another 'smart comment', but then I realised he was indicating the inside pocket of his blazer. 'A little something I made for myself.'

'Is that your spray dye?'

'No way man, the problem with that stuff is you end up getting covered in the muck yourself if you try to use it on someone.'

Sounded like a sensible observation, I hadn't thought too deeply about the repercussions of using the dye spray. It hadn't come to mind as something I could have used in my carpark encounter with Gary Blower, and that had been the only situation, so far, where I might have had cause to use it. Spray dye was just another instance of me rashly stampeding ahead, making a decision on behalf of the team, without thinking to ask their advice first.

'It's just an aftershave spray I came across, which has a fairly powerful spray nozzle. With a little bit of 'needle engineering', I've modified the nozzle so that the aftershave comes out in a jet rather than a spray. Theoretically my adjustment makes it illegal, but that would need to be tested in court. If it ever came to that.'

'Is it because you like your attackers to smell nice?' I joked.

'Have you ever accidentally sprayed aftershave in your eyes? No? Yes?' He waited for me to nod my acceptance of his point.

'Also, if ever I am stopped by the law, with this in my pocket, what can they charge me with? Carrying a fragrant weapon?' A big grin on his face, seeing the logic of what he had just said 'striking home' with me.

'Mal.' I said, 'You have far more experience than me in a lot of things, that I am only now coming to realise. I would truly appreciate it if, in future, you would offer your advice and check me when you think I am going down the wrong path.'

'Gotcha Boss,' he said. 'I'll cover your back, and I'll try to do it when the ladies aren't looking.' Big smile on his face again. He meant Sal and Jules, of course.

'And please, it's Chilli, not Boss.' I added.

'Chilli, yes Boss.'

I smiled; what else could I do?

We pulled up at 'Goodfellow's Heath Centre' ten minutes later, just about five minutes before our pre-agreed meet-up time at 6 pm. Parking was no problem; the old Bank had a small pull-in area off the road that would accommodate three, or maybe even four, regular-size cars. Mine was the only car there at present. Goodfellow's gym apparently wasn't that busy this time in the early evening, and Goodfellow's car - I had no idea what he drove - must have been parked elsewhere. Sloppy detective work on my part again, I chided myself, I should have known what Goodfellow drove and even what his registration number was. It wasn't an issue now, but nonetheless, it was sloppy.

I got out of the Evoque, there were a few spots of rain in the air, but nothing worth worrying about. Certainly not umbrella weather, just that penetratingly damp, miserable sort of weather, that makes you wish you'd stayed at home.

I looked across at Mal on the other side of my car; no smiles now. We were both feeling the tension in the air. Nodding to each other, we walked up to the double doors that would have been the main entrance to the old Bank.

There was a sheet of paper sellotaped to the door, 'Closed for business.' It was probably intended for anyone else who might have turned up to visit the gym while Goodfellow was entertaining me.

I pressed the doorbell and waited. Pressed again, waiting for someone to come to open the doors. No one came, but there was a loud metallic click, the sound of a door lock being automatically disengaged. The door on the left remained closed, but the one on the right opened an inch or so, inviting us to push it further and gain entry. I assume this was some sort of a safety precaution, probably a remnant of the building's security system dating back to when it was a bank.

It was a double entrance. Two paces past the first set of doors, there were a second set of heavy solid wood swing doors with clear glass upper panels that allowed visitors to see through into the main foyer area of the reception. The space between both sets of doors was carpeted with coconut shell coloured and heavily worn coir matting, again I thought, a leftover remnant of the building's old banking role.

We walked through into the main entrance area. The front door hadn't fully closed behind us; it stayed in that part-opened position, it would need someone to physically walk up and push it closed. I purposefully hadn't pulled it shut when we entered, leaving it partly open seemed a sensible, cautious position for our situation, best having an unimpeded route out of the place if we needed to leave in a hurry.

The reception area featured what looked to be well-cared-for parquet flooring and dark brown three-quarter wood panelled walls.

It must have been there before Goodfellow converted the old Bank into a gym, and he obviously recognised the positive visual and practical value of keeping it well cared for and, in the case of the parquet flooring, clean and nicely polished.

The walls were painted in that parchment white emulsion that seems to be a common choice for most of the banks I have ever visited. Strips of yellowing Sellotape hung, here and there, on the walls, where notices or pictures had been removed in the past.

What 'solid confidence' the sturdiness of the bank building had acquired, over its years of service, was now lost in the dust, grime, and the newly acquired Sellotape of its current role. With a bit of care and attention and a good scrubbing, it felt as if this place might still be made to look quite smart. Still, I wasn't there to survey the decor.

Goodfellow was there waiting for us in the foyer. His smile made me think of a used car salesman about to pounce on an ageing prospect. He was resting back against a tall, solid-looking, dark wooden and obviously vintage reception desk. Probably a remnant again from the building's previous role. An old-fashioned black Bakelite telephone stood on the side of the desk, the type of phone with a circular dial for dialling the numbers, but I thought this was probably just, for effect, a bit of leftover decoration. Once again, either Goodfellow or someone with influence over the design layout of the reception area had, at some time, given careful thought in choosing what few bits of functional, and decorative, furniture were to be left in place.

There was a solid-looking three-legged table close to the reception desk, on which sat what looked like a dishevelled pile of well-thumbed fitness magazines, but there was little else in the reception foyer to indicate that this was a fitness centre.

I turned my attention back to the man facing us. Although I vaguely remembered seeing Goodfellow a few times when I had visited Corley Rugby Club in the past, I had never actually met with him in person, and the only time we had spoken previously was at our 'shouted chat', the other day, when he refused to let me into the gym and, of course, the subsequent phone call we had incurred.

I took a moment to 'take in' the person who had been the cause of so much stress and anxiety for Haley. In my simple language, the villain of the story.

He was about my height, which would have put him at around five foot ten or eleven. With long dark curly hair that hung in (I think they are termed) 'dreadlocks' down to just past the zipped neck of a turquoise and black - hooded tracksuit top. It was obvious that, with his small, trimmed moustache and fashioned beard, together with what looked like a liberal use of eye make-up, he was trying to portray an image of himself fashioned on the pirate captain 'Jack

Sparrow', the Johnny Depp character from the film series of 'Pirates of the Caribbean'.

What a twat!

Still, here I was with a self-deluded image of myself as a Jack Reacher-type character from one of Lee Child's books, so I probably was not the right person to challenge, or criticise, someone else for their attempts to establish a chosen persona.

He glanced past me at Mal, but not before I noticed a slight frown on his face that disappeared almost immediately, someone else being present hadn't been in his plans, which meant he needed to rethink things a little, weigh up the odds. Just a moment's hesitation, then he pushed himself away from the reception desk and took a step towards me, holding out his hand for me to shake.

'Hi Chilli Pepper - Yes?' A slight hesitation then, 'I can call you Chilli, can't I? I don't think we have met before.'

'Chilli will do fine.'

I took his hand for a brief shake, it wasn't much of a shake, he had something of a limp wrist. 'Jack Sparrow piece of acting' again, I thought. But maybe I was being hypercritical.

'And your friend?'

'Hi, I'm Mal; I'm just along for the ride.'

Mal kept his hands in his pockets I noticed and neither of them offered to shake hands with each other.

All three of us shared pretend smiles, the sincerity of which wouldn't have convinced a three-year-old.

We stood there for a long moment as if waiting for something to happen before I broke through the silence.

'I mentioned to Mal that I was thinking of joining a gym and wanted to take a look at your place. He, by coincidence, was thinking he needed to sort out his beer gut, and we thought maybe we could find somewhere we could both join?'

'Sure, why not? Let's see what we have here that might be an acceptable training programme for you both.'

As the parody of friendly ignorance continued, I took a glance around to see what, if any, of Goodfellow's communication devices might be in the vicinity. I was pretty sure Mal was doing the same. Nothing was in sight. There was what appeared to be the shape of a phone in Goodfellow's shirt pocket. That would be something of a challenge to get to.

'Let's go on through into the gym. We can take a look at the equipment as we talk. A good place to start our chat from.' Goodfellow said, holding out his hand to direct us through the partitioned wall into the main training area.

I walked through the open doorway into the gym, Mal close behind and Goodfellow bringing up the rear, closing the door behind us.

The first thing that hit me was the sour, musty smell of the room. It was clear that the care shown in keeping the front foyer area clean and tidy had not been carried across into the main training area, where the miasma of stale sweat lingered in the air.

There were six or so of what would be termed 'fitness machines', Exercise Bikes, Treadmills, a Rowing Machine, and something, which I think is called an Elliptical Trainer, a device I would definitely avoid if I were ever to seriously consider joining a gym. All of the machines were positioned about the room to make it appear to be well equipped, and all looked tired, grubby and as if they were nearing the end of their intended life cycle.

'These are our 'self-trainers', Goodfellow told us. 'And over here are our free weights, dumbbells, medicine balls, Indian clubs, and the such.'

He drew our attention to a couple of small, narrow benches next to two weight support racks, bars, weight plates, and a collection of other equipment, all to one side of a stacked pile of four or five rubber mats. What you would expect to see in any gym, I suppose, something of a mixed assortment.

The rubber mats had probably seen better days, repaired with black rubber tape that had rolled back in places and was peeling away at the edges. Again all looked grubby and in need of a thorough cleaning before they were next used.

'So, there you have it, Mr Pepper - sorry, Chilli - as you see, there is a wide assortment of equipment. All very nice, but unless you have a sensible training plan to work to, nowhere near as effective in achieving your fitness goals as they need to be for maximum benefit.' He waved his hands around as if to take in all of his equipment.

'But what we need to do is work out a personalised plan for both of you, Gentlemen. So what is it you want?' His voice changed from the soft, semi-lisping tone as a hardness came into its presence.

'What is it you want? Cut the crap. What is it you really want?' he snapped, no longer any pretence of friendliness.

I stared back at him, readying myself for whatever was to happen next.

'My friend Mal here needs to borrow your phone for a couple of minutes to remove some of the files you have stored there. Specifically, video material of you abusing Haley White.'

'I'm afraid I have no idea what you are talking about, my dear.' His dandy way of talking re-emerged in the way he spoke and overtly gestured with his hands.

'I think someone has been feeding you a wicked story about me.' His lips quivered, and a false smile broke onto his face as he spoke.

'Can I assume that this Haley woman has made some incredibly untrue accusations with regard to my behaviour?'

'Stop the pretence. We both know what I am talking about - you have in your possession a video showing your sick and perverted activities with a lady that you had covertly drugged.'

He smiled and gave one of his Jack Sparrow flippant waves as if brushing away an annoying fly.

'A complete untruth. Covertly hey? A fancy word and a flagrant and abusive defamation of my character. I can assure you I have no such recordings of whatever it is you are falsely accusing me of.'

I hadn't expected him to admit it, so I tried a little bluff of my own.

"We have seen the video - Haley showed it to us and the message in which you sent it to her.'

We hadn't, of course; I couldn't even have told him how the message had been sent. Obviously something Haley had access to had she not deleted it, but whatever the means used, we lacked that one bit of evidence that possibly could have been used to threaten Goodfellow. However, he wasn't to know that.

He changed his tact immediately; gone was the soft, flamboyant 'Jack Sparrow' imitation act, and back came the nastier blunt hardness in his voice and facial expression.

'Who's to say - even if you have this video - that it is me in the film? Are there any pictures actually showing my face?' He knew there weren't. 'What have you got? Just supposing you have what you say you have, is there anything to show that I am one of the people participating? And even if you could show I was there, who's to say that the bitch wasn't gagging for it? And who's to say it wasn't her who came on to me?'

'Perhaps,' he added, 'She wanted a bit of white meat for a change?'

The bastard had it all figured out. He knew there was nothing we had, in the way of proof, that it had been a date rape.

'Let's look at this another way.' The Jack Sparrow voice was back, along with the flippant hand-waving gestures. 'If, and I say - if - I were to have happened to have come across such a video showing this young lady enjoying herself. It might be something she might regret and possibly wish to pay a sum of money for me to help out and have it removed from existence.'

A change of ploy, the bastard was now looking to be paid for getting rid of the video.

I thought I would give him 'a little rope' to see what it was financially he thought he could make to benefit from this situation.

'If that were the case, what would you be seeking to gain from this?'

'Well, I do feel that I am the injured party here. All of these wild accusations of rape and such. I have my reputation to maintain; then there is the possible damage to my business. Accusations of this nature could affect my business. People would not want to visit my gym if they felt they might be at risk. And, of course, the damage to my image, wild rumours of such lies being circulated are bound to be bad for my image.'

'What a load of bullshit.' Mal erupted - Even I was somewhat taken aback by Mal's challenge. I think it was the first time I had ever heard him swear. In this company, it wouldn't be the last, I was sure.

'I think a financial recompense might be something that we should be considering if - as you say - I were to help in making this video disappear forever.'

'What are we talking about here? What is your price?' I asked.

'Well, if we were to include a small allowance for my friend to help compensate for his terrible head injury, I think rounding it up to say a thousand pounds would be a fair amount to offset the problems Mrs White has caused with her ridiculous accusations.'

'And what is there to say that you wouldn't keep a copy and use it in the future to top up your blackmail pot?' I asked.

'Blackmail pot?' He laughed. 'I can assure you I am a man of my word. One thousand pounds, and this goes away forever.'

'Go fuck yourself.'

'So sorry to hear we are unable to reach an amenable solution. If there is no financial benefit to be gained for my trying to help out here, I guess there is only Plan B to fall back on.'

Goodfellow pulled on a small red cord, which hung from the ceiling next to the free weights - probably some sort of emergency safety warning device. There was no audible sound, but it must have rung out somewhere because it was then that Barry Spencer came into the room carrying two wooden 'Indian Clubs', one in each hand, the clubs were the old-fashioned wooden type that looked like a coconut on the end of a walking stick. From the look on Spencer's face, it was apparent that he had been looking forward to our reunion.

It was good to see that he was still bound up with bandages that wrapped around his head and holding some padding over his damaged left ear. He was, I could see, still feeling some discomfort, his two bloodshot eyes squinting as he made his rush towards me.

I had no time to think, I readied myself to offset his rush. If I had time to think I had made a mistake in walking into the lion's den, my bowels would have turned to water. But I didn't. In that split second, the one thought I had was, 'Shit, is this where these fuckers get to even the score? A couple of unarmed 'old guys' against two younger twats armed with clubs?'

Mal moved first; he had already slipped his aftershave spray into his hand. He moved two steps across the room and sprayed the perfume directly into Spencer's eyes. Spencer screamed.

'You bastard, you fuckin bastard.' he cried, trying to rub his eyes, but not able to do so without dropping the clubs.

I took advantage of the distraction and loosened the stool leg out from the cuff of my sleeve, and with a backhanded side sweep, brought it down across the other side of Spencer's head to where the padding was. He went down like a sack of potatoes, 'out to the world'. This time, he could find his own bloody way to A&E.

273

I turned to face Goodfellow. The blood had drained from his face as he realised the predicament, he was now in. His plans, whatever they had been, had just been turned upside down, and he was literally up 'Shit Creek'.

Just then, there was an almighty crash from the front door of the gym and the sound of running feet. My immediate thought was that it must be some of Goodfellow's pals that I hadn't counted on.

I backed up to Mal, part-shielding him behind me and my deadly stool leg. I wasn't feeling particularly brave, just a sense of guilt and bloody responsible for landing us in this mess.

I reached into my pocket and pulled out the dye spray. It came out easily. I had half expected to snag it on my pocket, but luck was with me, and gripping it in my left hand, I pointed it directly at Goodfellow's face.

A spray in one hand, a stool leg in the other - my pal behind me and my foes in front - just like the final 'stand-off' scene in a film like 'The Sting'.

Then, the door between the reception area and the gym flew open as though someone had given it an almighty shove with their foot - which they probably had - and in dashed two Donald Trumps, a Kim Jong Un, and a Boris Johnson. Well, not really the actual characters themselves, just four men, or what I assumed were men, in white hazard suits, wearing latex politician's face masks and blue nitrile gloves and shoe covers.

The first guy, a Boris Johnson, looked over in my direction and said in a deep, mellow voice, 'No worries, Mr Pepper, the cavalry's here! Though by the looks of things, once again, it seems like you didn't need us.'

I wasn't sure what he meant by 'once again'. Not that it mattered much at that time.

After a brief scuffle with Goodfellow, two of them, the Donald Trumps, had managed to roughly grab Goodfellow and, with his arms forced behind him, had brought him heavily down onto his knees, on the paint-sealed concrete floor, next to the loosely stacked cast iron plate weights.

Goodfellow had a look of sheer terror on his face, and a dark patch was spreading around the front of his tracksuit bottoms where he had lost control of his bladder.

'Go tell her we have him.' The guy in the Boris Johnson mask said, and Kim Jong Un disappeared back out of the door they had just burst through.

'We've been following you for a couple of days now. Waiting for you to make your move, earn your money, and get your hands on the original copy of the video that Goodfellow took.'

Earn my money? Where did that one come from?

Kim Jong Un returned seconds later with another Boris Johnson. This one also kitted out in the white hazard suit, latex mask, gloves, and shoe covers, was of slighter build than the other 'politicians', and I was pretty certain I knew who it was under the covering disguise.

'Have you got what you came looking for, Mr Pepper?' Definitely, a female voice I had heard before.

'Mal?' I asked, looking towards him.

'Not yet. I need his mobile for a few minutes.' Mal said.

'Kim.' She said, and the character with the Kim Jong Un mask walked over to where Goodfellow was being held and picked the mobile phone out from the pocket of his tracksuit bottoms.

'The dirty bastards pissed on it.' Kim said. I made out his broad Yorkshire accent.

'It's maybe an age-related thing.' I said. A poorly timed piece of misplaced humour given the intensity of the situation. It was inappropriate, I suppose; no one laughed, and everyone ignored me. I wasn't surprised.

'Wipe it on his top and pass it over to the gentleman with Mr Pepper,' the male Boris said.

I couldn't make out Boris' accent; the mask must have muffled it somewhat, but from the deep timbre of his voice and from the patch of skin I noticed around the lower edge of his mask, it was obvious that he was a black guy. I, of course, might have been entirely wrong. I had never actually met him before, but I surmised this was probably Sam White, Haley's husband, with some of his work pals or maybe some of the guys from the rugby club - it didn't matter. No prizes for my guesswork; after all, who else could it be?

'The phone is yours now – do you need to keep it, or just smash it?'

'I just need it for a couple of minutes.' Mal said, taking the phone. 'Ah, that makes it all that much easier; it's a fingerprint recognition one.'

He handed it back to Kim Jong Un. 'Get him to press his finger here.' Pointing at the button designed to provide access to the device.

'What happens now?' I asked the male Boris.

'You do your magic to clean out the shit this fuckpig has on his phone; we teach him never to do it again and even up the score with him a little.'

Goodfellow let out a low, lingering moan. Then 'No Chilli, no, please no, please, don't do this Chilli, it's a mistake she wanted me to do it.'

This guy really was a moron if he thought trying to blame Haley would help him escape what he had coming.

'We can't be a party to anything that will put us at odds with the law.' I said. 'My friend here is a practicing law officer, and I need to ensure his position is not compromised whatsoever.'

'Very kind of you Chilli,' muttered Mal. 'But I don't think we're calling the shots here.'

'You don't have to worry, Mr Pepper. You and your friend will not be implicated at all.' The male Boris said. Definitely a touch of inherited Caribbean twang coming out in his accent.

He was, obviously, the one in-charge of this little group of counterfeit politicians and was certainly the one directing events.

'When your friend has what he wants, you will be free to leave. Then you do the right thing and call for an ambulance to come here, damn quick, as you go.'

'An ambulance for what injuries you are intending to cause to Goodfellow here?'

'No, no. The ambulance is for the poor sod you hit with your club.'

'It's not a club; it's a stool leg.' I protested.

'Something you picked up here? Or something you brought with you?'

'I brought it with me.' I said, but I had just begun to see his reasoning. Whatever I called it, if this ever went to trial, my stool leg would definitely be categorised as a club.

Mal had been quietly beavering away, working at whatever he needed to do - downloading Goodfellow's files and, I supposed, installing a 'worm' of some sort that would cleanse out whatever it subsequently came into contact with.

'I am sure Mr Goodfellow will want to accompany his friend to the hospital. Two birds with one stone.' He said. 'Hey, Mrs Boris, you get that? Two birds - one stone.' Then, they all, the masked intruders that is, broke into peals of laughter.

'How did you know we would be here at Goodfellow's gym this afternoon?' I asked, genuinely interested in how they had managed to time their appearance to coincide with our visit.

The female Boris walked over and held up a pair of secateurs in her blue nitrile gloved hand.

'The guys have been following you for a couple of days now, they spotted the 'home help,' she gestured towards the prostrate Spencer, 'trying to accost you in the supermarket car park and were about to step in. But it seemed like you had it all under control.' I felt there were no tears in her eyes under that mask now. She had a purpose in mind, and I could see there was little Mal or I would be able to do to dissuade her from whatever she was intending.

'Time to go Chilli.' Mal said, taking a small plastic bag from his pocket, removing a wet wipe, and giving the phone a thorough wipe down before passing it back to Kim.

Kim just dropped it onto the painted concrete gym floor, picked up one of the heavier weight-plates and slammed it down, edge-on, onto the mobile phone, smashing it into a useless mess.

'Time for you and your friend to leave now Mr Pepper.' The male Boris said in a cold, calm voice.

'No, no, please.' Goodfellow whimpered.

I knew there was nothing we could do to change matters, but it still didn't seem right to be walking away from something I felt uncomfortable with.

'Tango asked me to say you needed to meet up for a drink again sometime soon.' I said as a parting shot.

Boris said nothing in reply.

As we made our way out of the gym, Mal holding my arm as if guiding me through the doors, he spoke quietly to me so as not to be overheard.

'Listen, Chilli, I spotted something I think we need to look at, away from here. Something that, if I'm right, will convince you that this guy Goodfellow deserves whatever he gets and more.'

Chapter 24 - The Journey Back

Tuesday 7th/2, early evening continued

We walked in silence back to the car, both, I'm sure, feeling a bit dazed by the events that had just taken place. I certainly was.

I 'zap' unlocked the doors, and we both climbed into our seats in stunned silence. The rain had stopped, not that I can say I noticed that then. The dull weather seemed appropriate though, it matched both our moods.

'Phone 999 Mal.' I said in almost a whisper.

The silence lingered on for a few moments, then Mal answered.

'I will, Chilli, but I think you should take a look at this first.'

He opened up his iPad and spent a couple of seconds tapping away at the on-screen keyboard.

'I wanted you to see this, and I didn't want that masked crew to see what I had found. Otherwise, things might have gotten out of hand.'

He turned the screen to me and showed me the display. There were four files listed. The fourth file was titled 'Haley'; Mal opened it briefly to show it was the video Goodfellow had taken of himself abusing Haley.

Mal then flicked over and opened the third file listed as 'Debbie'.

I thought - 'Oh my god, no!'

It was as I had dreaded. A woman in Goodfellow's gym being sexually used in a number of different ways, he made as much inappropriate use of the training equipment there as could be devised by a sick mind. From the 'zombie' way in which she moved and the blank look on her face, it was apparent that she was either under the influence of alcohol or some sort of medication. 'Medication' meaning date-rape drug.

Knowing what we did of Goodfellow's track record, I was certain that she had used the same date-rape drug as he had used on Haley, either GHB or Rohypnol.

'The dirty bastard. He drove one to commit suicide - invited himself to her funeral - then, the same day, looked for a replacement for his perverted needs at Debbie's wake. The dirty, sick bastard.'

'Certainly looks that way. I really hope they do cut his gonads off.' Mal said.

'Call 999.' I told Mal. 'But only call for an ambulance. Tell them a man has hurt his head in the gym. Leave it for the ambulance crew to notify the police when they find whatever they do when they get there.'

'That's what I was thinking.' Mal said.

I fastened my seatbelt, started the car up, checked the road was clear, and pulled out from the parking space as Mal made the 999 call. Again, we drove in silence, our minds running through the events that had so rapidly just taken place, replaying them over and over again. To me, it seemed like something I had watched happen rather than something I had been a part of. I think the aftershock of the whole incident was just beginning to hit me.

Mal broke the silence, bringing me back into the present.

'I trust the two Borises and the fake politicians will have finished whatever it was they were intending to do and will have cleared the gym before the emergency services arrive.'

'I guess this means we will have to miss out on going for a beer with Goodfellow tonight, then?' I said, trying to break us both out of the shock we were feeling.

'No, I don't think that was on the cards for us anyway. If the cavalry hadn't arrived when they did, I think we might have needed to settle matters with Goodfellow ourselves.'

'What do you think he intended to do to us?' I wondered aloud.

'Well, I'm pretty sure me being there threw a brick in his works. If you were on your own, as he had intended, he would have wanted to teach an old man like you a lesson for sticking your nose into something that was none of your business. A punishment for interfering in his sexual pastimes. It messed his plans up when he saw there were two of us. But then again - 'the plans of mice and men' - I think he must have still fancied his chances, looked at us, and thought - a couple of old fogies like them - What can they do? I'll get Blowjob to even his score, break a few bones, and throw in some threats of what would happen if we caused any more problems and that we would then drop out of the picture. I guess if questioned by the police, he would have put any injuries we incurred down as self-inflicted while inappropriately using his gym equipment.'

'I reckon you're right. If it ever did involve the police and he was backed into a corner, there's no doubt he would put the blame onto his pet gorilla, Spencer. Claim he was trying to get his revenge on me for putting him in hospital the other day. That shite Goodfellow has zero morals or feelings of loyalty, and I'm pretty certain he would not hesitate in throwing his pal to the wolves if he thought it would save his skin or benefit him in any other way.'

We drove on in silence for a few minutes, both reflecting on what had just happened.

Then Mal dropped his bombshell.

'Well, it was a good job I recorded the whole thing on this' he said, slipping his hand into the inside pocket of his blazer and taking out a small, slim black device, which I initially thought looked like a cross between a credit card and an extremely thin mobile phone.

'You recorded it on your phone.' I said.

'Not my phone. This is my SMT digital voice-activated recorder, one of the best on the market.'

'You cunning so and so. Where did that come from? You never said anything about having a voice recorder. So, when did you switch it on? Did you capture the whole thing?'

'An awful lot of questions there, boss. It came from my own kit of security devices, some of which actually belong to the NCA, and I have been issued with. But I would appreciate it if you didn't spread that information outside of the team; I'm pretty sure I might get a few awkward questions from the 'high-ups' if it came to their attention that I was using it in my work for you. I switched it on as we got out of the car when we arrived at Goodfellow's gym.'

'And it's been running the whole time since we got there?'

'You got it. It is voice activated, and anyway, the battery lasts forever. So it got the lot. It's even capturing our conversation now.' He added, moving the small button on the top edge of the device to switch it off.

'Bloody hell. You're a star, Mal. We need to get everyone on the team one of those.'

'Wouldn't be a bad idea. I shouldn't really be using this one for private work.'

We drove on in silence for a short while, running matters through our minds. Then, I broke the silence.

'Mal, I don't think we should tell anyone, outside of the team, about the Debbie video. There is nothing to be gained from letting anyone else know of its existence, and it will cause so much unnecessary distress.'

'I agree, but I think we need to speak to the rest of the team and get their opinion and agreement before making that decision. You will have no friends if they think you are still trying to hide things from them.'

'Of course. Can you give them a call while I drive? Tell them we are both safe and the problem has been addressed - without going into any detail. They will both be sitting on the edge of their seats, waiting to hear what has happened. Best ask them to meet us when we get back, then we can let them know how things went.'

'If you don't mind, I'll ask them to meet us in your local pub, Chilli. I am in dire need of a beer. I've got to tend to that beer gut you told Goodfellow I was thinking of working off in his gym'.

'Damn right.' I agreed. 'I could murder a Guinness.'

'Or two.'

'You will be popping out of bed for a pee all night.'

It started as a smile, then morphed into two old men giggling, and from there to two old men laughing raucously - me having to pull the car over into a layby. It was just like a dam had broken, and the pent-up stress we had both been feeling was finally being released.

'That was a close one.'

'Yup - It bloody well was,' I agreed, 'too bloody close.'

Chapter 25 - Poor Old Goebbels

Tuesday 7th/2 - circa 8 pm

We got back to the village in less than an hour, even allowing for our laughter break.

Sal, Jules, and Truffle were waiting in The Queens Crown pub and had already taken occupancy of a small table in the Snug. Either Jules or Sal had bought their drinks, and a pint of Guinness and a bottle of San Miguel with its glass stood waiting for us. Both were sitting in the corner closest to the log fire and had taken off their outer coats, which were now draped over the backs of their chairs.

When they saw us, both ladies jumped to their feet and held their arms wide apart for us in welcome. Their chairs toppled backwards with the weight of their coats, but no one bothered to pick them up at that moment. Every one of us wearing our broadest smiles, part with relief and part with joy and, yes, pride at having successfully completed our first client undertaking. Even though it hadn't quite been the type of work we were expecting when we first entered into this case.

There were long lingering hugs all around and even a trace of tears of joy and relief in both Sally's and Julie's eyes.

I have to admit to a sense of dampness in my own tear ducts, but I hid it well. Still quite an emotional reunion.

Truffle added to the greeting, yapping and doing her excited little tail-waggling shuffle, jumping up at my legs for attention, then rolling over onto her back to have her tummy rubbed, which, of course, both Mal and I obliged her with.

We took off our coats and hung them up on the coat stand in the corner by the door. The ladies picked their coats and chairs up from where they had toppled over and passed them over to us to hang up with ours. Then we all sat down, me with Truffle resting contentedly on my lap.

I began telling the story of our visit to Goodfellow's gym, step by step, so that I missed nothing of note from what had happened. Occasionally, Mal came forward to clarify or explain in a little more detail something that I had brushed over, not thinking it needed clarifying.

I told them of how Mal had coolly stepped forward between Spencer and me to spray him in the eyes with aftershave, temporarily blinding the moron and distracting him from his revenge attack on me. Mal looked down a little embarrassed, I think by my portrayal of his heroic intervention.

'And don't underplay the way you stood in front of me when we thought we were going to be on the losing side -

when the cavalry arrived.' Mal put in. 'Because I won't. I owe you one, Chilli.'

'You owe me nothing.' I said. 'I think we both know each other a lot better now, my friend.' And I meant it. From work pals to best friends in just one afternoon.

'Oh, I do wish I'd been there,' Jules said. 'I feel like I have been a part of the story for so much of the time, only to miss out on the final chapter.'

'Don't be so hard on yourself, Jules. Everyone had their part to play, and you were vital in our understanding of the issues with Haley's sad experience and so important in making me realise what a bombastic and sexist twit I had been in my earlier behaviour, in not being completely open with the team. I now accept that we are all a part of the same team 'toolbox', and when a specific task is identified, it is important to choose the right tool, regardless of gender, to best achieve the intended outcome.'

I could see that my words did little to change her feeling of missing out on the excitement, but none of us could have predicted how things were going to turn out when we did finally confront Goodfellow, and the choice we had made was right and fitted well in my toolbox analogy.

In the back of my mind, though, was a feeling that with one of the women there, in Goodfellow's gym, we might have worried more for their safety and behaved with a little more caution in our final approach.

'Enough of this thinking about what might have been - I'm starving. Have you ladies eaten?' They both shook their heads.

'No? Then who fancies a curry?' We were lucky; there were two Indian restaurants in our village, both were good, and both just a short walking distance from the pub.

'We will have to drop Truffle off first, can't take her in.' Sal reminded me.

'Course not.' I said. 'Not a problem. I'll drop her off in the car, then walk back and meet you in The Chakra Palace. I can have another Guinness then, not having to drive home.'

Sal smiled, she knew my preference was for one of the special dishes in the other restaurant that wasn't an option on the menu at the Palace, but The Chakra Palace had been hers and our kids' favourite from way back.

And the Palace would be a good choice, there was more space, and we would be able to discuss our adventure a little more in detail without being overheard by people sitting too close by.

So, all in agreement, we finished our drinks and put on our coats.

'Nice to see you and Wolf again, Mr Pepper.' Called Jason as we were leaving. 'Don't leave it so long next time. I miss seeing Truffle.'

'We won't.' I said. 'See you.'

Sal, leading the way out through the main exit door, looked back at me in a caring way and asked, 'Do you need the toilet before we go.'

'Bloody comedian.' I responded. And we made our way outside.

I drove Truffle back home, quickly nipped to the loo, gave Wolf and the cats some food to keep them happy, and set off at a quick walking pace back to join the others at the Palace. The whole episode taking less than thirty minutes.

When I got there, the team were already seated in a corner location set back a little from the other diners in the restaurant. An Ideal spot, the gentle Indian background music and general noise of people enjoying their meals meant we had a modicum of privacy in which we could talk if we kept the level of our voices down a little.

Sally had already ordered a round of 'starters' for us before we got around to choosing our main courses, and I didn't hesitate in putting on my reading glasses and tucking into an onion bhaji literally within seconds of sitting down.

Jules insisted we talk them through the whole event again, starting from when I collected Mal right through until when we arrived back at The Queens Crown. I figured it was a part of the conditioning that resulted from her years of having a police background. A way of ensuring she had all of the facts necessary to piece the scene together in her mind and ensure we missed nothing.

This time, Mal took the lead, I was too busy eating my onion bhaji - I think the excitement of reliving the story had worked to stimulate my appetite. He retold the whole story, emphasising how grimy the inside of the gym building and the equipment was. I couldn't have said that I had paid too much attention to the cleanliness of the premises. Mal added that it was an unsanitary tip and that he would need a bath when he finally got home if he wasn't to go down with some illness or other. Finally, he brought his narrative to the point where he had accessed the files from Goodfellow's phone and implanted a 'worm' to clean out all traces of the recordings in it.

That was the most important piece of the news, I thought, and Mal, I felt, had underplayed his part there.

I told both Sal and Jules of the 'blinder' Mal had played by recording the whole episode in the gym on his voice recorder.

'If you ladies really want to listen in on the whole interchange that took place in the gym, I'm sure Mal will be able to let you listen to his recording.'

'Not now, maybe later once this whole thing has settled down, and we know if we are going to be roped into this whole circus. Mal, how confident are you that he will not be able to access and use those videos ever again?' Sally asked.

'I know my job, he won't be able to access them ever again - even if he wanted to, which I seriously doubt he ever will, after whatever the 'politicians' have done to him.'

'What do you think they will have done?' Jules asked.

'I'm pretty sure Haley had something in mind with those secateurs she was carrying, but I think that is where we are going to need you Jules to employ your skills. Speak with your contacts to find out. But I suggest you leave it a couple of days, before making a few very discrete enquiries. You have your contacts in the police?'

'Yes, and I also have a few contacts at Coventry's A&E as well. That's where they would have taken him. Bugger leaving it a few days, I'll find out tonight. I can do it without stirring up any problems. There are enough people 'in the know' who owe me a few favours.'

'Please, Jules, leave it until tomorrow. Let's keep this as 'low-key' as we possibly can.' I asked.

'You've got my word, Chilli, tomorrow it is, but it will be tomorrow morning for certain.'

Chapter 26 - The Next Day

After finishing our meal and another drink each, we all walked back, in a silly, joyful, chatty way, to my house. Both Sal and I had drunk too much alcohol for either of us to risk driving Mal back to his house or for Jules to attempt driving to her home in Kenilworth. So the outcome, understandably, was that Jules and Mal became our 'houseguests' for the night.

That wasn't a problem; it was a nice way of ending the evening. We had a couple of spare bedrooms, now that the kids were away doing 'their things', and it meant we could all listen in when Jules tapped up her contacts the next morning to learn of Goodfellow's fate.

We showed them both, Jules and Mal, to their allocated rooms. I suggested Jules use my daughter Jane's room. The bed and room was smaller than my son's, where Mal was to be accommodated. But the decor and 'girl's things' - left around seemed to be more appropriate for a lady than the detritus left around in our son Marcus's room, something that we hadn't yet got around to tidying up, or putting away, since his last visit home.

At least Mal's room was ensuite, so he could shower to his heart's content to remove any of the potential illness-making filth he felt he had had to endure at Goodfellow's gym.

Sal volunteered to tell our guests that they should not be too alarmed if they heard any noises on the landing at night. 'Our bedroom isn't ensuite, and Chilli tends to need two or three pees to get him through the night, especially if he has had a few beers.'

There goes any credibility I might have retained, I thought, but I left it at that. No point in any 'tit for tat' humour that late in the evening - best keep a snide retort for some time of my choosing in the future.

It must have been gone 9 am the next morning before the first sounds of anyone waking became apparent. Contrary to the norm, I had slept right through, not needing the toilet at all until I finally woke,

'You'd better get down and let Truffle out into the garden for a pee.' Sal announced.

'What's wrong with you going?' I asked. But I didn't expect a reply and didn't get one. So I went down, let Truffle out, and fed both cats - my normal daily routine.

I wasn't feeling too bad considering the three or four pints of Guinness and an Indian Madras Curry I had partaken of the night before.

I went back upstairs, showered, and toileted before getting up properly, getting dressed, and tidying up my clothes from the night before.

I had slept like a log - though Sal later informed all of our guests, when they finally got up, that it was more like a log in a sawmill, with my snoring.

By around 10 am, everyone had finally got up, showered and whatever, and joined me for breakfast. I had thought it easiest for us all to go along to the Airfield Cafe for a full English Breakfast. It would have saved having to 'mess around' making breakfast at home, but I think we were all now starting to feel a few of the effects of last night's frivolity.

I busied myself feeding Truffle and the two cats ('White Cat' and 'Grey Cat') and waited to discuss with Sal, when she finally managed to come downstairs, about 'catering for our guests'. It was too early in the morning for me to think for myself.

Sally finally joined me, and we managed to lay out a breakfast of coffee - Weetabix and milk. It would have to do. Sal put out a saucer of blueberries that could be added to the breakfast bowls and 'tick the box' for one of the five-a-day fruits.

'Jules.' I said. 'Time to do a bit of investigative research?'

'Yep.' She said.

'She even sounds like you.' Mal said.

We all pretended we hadn't heard that remark.

'Let's go into the front room, where we can all sit down in comfort.' Sally said. 'Chilli lite the fire. Let's make it cosy.'

It didn't take long to get a fire going, and pretty soon, we had all found a seat where we could sit back in comfort for the latest update on the happenings of the day before.

'I think I'll phone the hospital first?' Jules told us. No one argued with that; it made sense to see the size of the problem before indicating to the police that we had any interest in the previous day's happenings.

She made her call, asking for one of her friends who worked as a doctor on the A&E side of Coventry University Hospital. He wasn't there. Apparently, he had been on duty last night and had set a pre-recorded message on his phone telling the caller to leave their number and that he would call back later today. Presumably, having been on duty the night before, his call back would be after he had had some sleep. Jules tried another number and, this time, got through to one of her other contacts.

'Hi Babs, it's Jules, how's things with you?'

The grey cat jumped up into her lap, and Julie fondled the cat's ear as she quietly listened to her friend's response.

Next followed a short spell of banter and laughter as both caught up on a few things that had occurred in their lives since last they spoke.

Fortunately, their last get-together had not been too long ago, so Jules artfully steered the conversations around to current times.

Barbara, or Babs as Jules knew her, was a senior nurse who worked in the A&E wing of the hospital. She hadn't been on duty last night but had heard 'on the grapevine' that there had been one unusual incident during yesterday's night shift. She had heard that, early in the evening, two men had been brought in, both suffering from injuries incurred at a gym in Bedworth.

One was a readmission. Apparently, she'd heard that he had received prior treatment at Warwick A&E a few days prior for a similar head injury that had resulted in severe concussion. The story was that both times, it was being described as self-inflicted while 'working out' with some Indian Clubs. She thought that it all sounded more than a little mysterious, first getting treated at Warwick, then there at Coventry, for what sounded like the same type of injury.

'Maybe the guy had been too embarrassed to return to the same hospital after doing the same thing to himself twice in a row!'

The other incident, she had been informed, was a partial castration. Hopefully, she told Julie they thought they might be able to repair the damage. Word was it might have occurred when the guy was using the rowing machine or something. Anyway, he was still in surgery, where they were attempting to put things back together again.

'I've heard that, because of the nature of the injury and the fact that two people had been taken into hospital from the same location at the same time, the police had become involved. But word was, they didn't seem to think anyone else was involved. Possibly the result of some altercation between the two men involved and were waiting for both of the injured parties to recover sufficiently for questioning.'

'Interesting', I thought, but still no closer to knowing how things might play out.

'Sounds like they had a go at cutting his tabs off. Great, serves him right.' Julie said, 'No clearer yet in knowing if we will be implicated at all in the revenge attack though.'

'It's what we all thought might happen.' Sal agreed, in quite a blunt off-hand way, and got up, leaving for the kitchen, where she began to make everyone a coffee.

'I'll see now what I can learn from my pals, 'the boys in blue' Julie told us.

'Wait until I've made the coffee.' Sally called back. 'I don't want to miss anything.'

'Don't worry, I'll wait until you're back. Sink or swim, we are in this together.'

She called one of her friends, a senior investigator in the NCA, told him she was interested in a reported incident from the previous evening, and asked him if he could get her an update on what the situation was. She implied that it might be linked to something she was looking at linked to a County Lines investigation that was taking place.

He promised to look into what information they had, if anything and would get back to her if anything came up.

Whoever she had been speaking to rang back within the hour. He told Julie that the local 'West Midlands Team' was looking into it, but the guys who had been injured, he was pretty sure, were victims of some drug-related trading. They were both known to the local police, and it was generally thought, by those looking into it, that the two parties, who were known for their prior involvement in handling drugs, had upset someone higher up in the supply chain and had been taught a lesson.

Neither of the victims had indicated that they intended to talk to the police, and the local guys, for their part, were not shedding any tears over these two jerks getting their comeuppance.

He was pretty sure the local police would not be spending much time digging into this much further, too many more deserving cases on their worklist.

'Looks like we might be clear of any 'blow-back' from the authorities.' Julie told us. 'I thought that might be the case, anyway; if things had gone pear-shaped, we would still have the taped conversations from the gym encounter to fall back on.'

'I also managed to download some other material from Goodfellow's phone when I had it. Incriminating evidence of his drug business that he might not want circulating or passing on to the local plod. I have a contact myself at the hospital - a guy I used to play Rugger with. He will be able to get a warning message to the 'Tooth Fairy' and let him know what's best for him going forward.'

'Tell your friend,' I put in, 'to tell Goodfellow I don't ever want to see him, or his pet ape Spencer, up at Corley Rugby Club ever again. He is to cut all ties, and if I ever see him thereabouts, I will let it be known about other crap he had on his phone.'

'What other stuff?' Jules asked in a delighted, expectant voice.

'Nothing, just trying to throw in a scarer.'

I know it was not strictly true, but I would let her and Jules know the full story later, when we had our full case

review, about the few things we had and would keep back -
on tape - against Goodfellow for 'insurance purposes'.

Chapter 27 - Surprise in the Post

Tuesday 14th Feb early morning

Valentine's Day!

So that was it. We had finished our first-ever Sap-laf-fea investigation, and while it was very different from the investigative undertakings we had originally intended as our line of work, it did have a satisfactory outcome.

There were one or two other outcomes that we hadn't directly anticipated. Word was beginning to spread, with no direct marketing on our part, that we were available to help people find lost or missing loved ones. I think the local police might have been instrumental in pointing a few people in our direction. We started to see a trickle of enquiries from friends and relatives of people in our circle of friends who had heard of what we were doing. Not a lot of enquiries yet and none involving the sort of nastiness in which we had just been involved, but enough to keep us active.

Still, it was getting to be a bit bothersome having to ring back people who had left messages on my answer phone at home or picking up 'please call me' notifications on my mobile. I know Julie was experiencing the same sort of problems. People had our details from the business cards I had printed before thinking things through at the outset. If business continued at this pace, we might need a part-time office administrator, I was beginning to think.

The big surprise came about a week after our visit to Goodfellow's gym.

Out of the blue, I received a thick envelope through the letterbox, addressed to 'To all my friends at the Sap-laf-fea'. It contained £500 in twenty-pound notes and a short unsigned Valentine's Day Card - A large red heart surrounded with party bubbles and inside a note that read;

'Don't get soppy; this is just a note from a black guy to say thank you - I know you do not ask for payment for the work you do, but hopefully, this will offset some of the costs you incurred in being a white knight.

If you ever need my help in the future, just call'.

A nice and unexpected touch, I thought, and put the money to one side to speak with Mal about getting us all one of those voice recording devices each.

'Essential equipment,' I told myself, 'for our line of work.'

I thought, 'I'll also reorder some new business cards and dump the old cards; Mal deserved his place to be there and shown on our business cards - Bugger the expense.'

I slipped on my Crocs, popped to the loo, then nipped out quickly with Truffle to the local newsagent to buy two Valentine cards.

www.ingramcontent.com/pod-product-compliance
Lightning Source LLC
Chambersburg PA
CBHW072003180726
48291CB00002BA/525